Rahi

Snigdha Jha

To the little girl who dreamed of writing

The Call

She lay on the soft, grassy bed, basking in the warm embrace, and wished the moment could last forever. The beautiful bird song in the distance and the sound of the soft breeze blowing through the trees were slowly fading into the gentle, rhythmic ring that rose from her side. As the ring grew louder, her arm stretched out in response to grab the source. With closed eyes, she fiddled with it, and a familiar voice screamed from the other end.

"Pack your bags, we're going to the Amazon!"

Furious at her childhood bestie for ruining her Saturday morning, she held back all the profanity in her vocabulary and responded as calmly as she could.

"Mehul, I am not doing this right now. We'll talk later. Bye."

"Wait! I'm serious. Everyone is on board. We just want you to agree."

Aaliyah sighed deeply and responded with an eerie calm. "Listen, Mehul, it's 6 a.m., it's a Saturday, and I'm trying really hard not to abuse you, so please don't push it. Let's talk later."

"FINE! Go back to sleep, grandma."

She flung the phone across the bed and buried her face in the pillow, attempting to recapture her dream. However, her mind was already preoccupied with questions about the absurd new plan her friends had concocted and thoughts of what to have for breakfast. Unable to retreat to dreamland, she decided to start her day early.

Feeling the familiar, all-consuming knot of anxiety coiling tightly within her chest, she reached for her phone with a sense of desperation. Without hesitation, she launched her trusted meditation app, selecting her favourite guided meditation. She closed her eyes, allowing the soothing voice of the meditation guide to envelope her, but the knot of anxiety remained stubbornly present. It refused to be untangled, holding her in its grip with a tenacity that left her feeling helpless and trapped. Desperate for relief, she abandoned the meditation and turned to binaural beats, hoping that the powerful sound waves would help to break the knot that had taken hold.

Struggling to concentrate on the gentle, rhythmic beats reverberating throughout her room, her mind wandered, contemplating how she had managed to maintain a more stable relationship with the perpetual knot in her heart than the majority of people in her life. It was one of those days when her mind refused to settle down. Eventually, she surrendered and rose from her bed.

"Good morning, Hex," she greeted her tortoise as she made her way to the kitchen. Hex looked up at her lazily and decided to retreat back into his shell. She cut up some melons and placed them on his plate. Grabbing her morning drink, she made her way to the dining room and settled by the window. The room was filled with the gentle glow of the sun's early light, filtering through the buttery curtains like a warm embrace.

While gazing out the window, a father and daughter caught her attention as they played with a lively Labrador puppy in the nearby park. The delightful moment brought back fond memories of her own childhood when she and her younger brother used to frequent the park, climbing trees and enjoying the swings when they weren't already taken by other kids.

She was lost in the sweet reverie, thinking of the good old days when her phone loudly buzzed on the table. She picked it up and saw the notification, "Dad's Birthday" staring back at her. A sense of reluctance and discomfort washed over her, and she hesitated to contact him.

"I should call him, but I can't. It's been weeks since we've talked," she muttered to herself.

Her inner critic chimed in, "You can't just wish him a happy birthday and not respond to his messages from last week, Aaliyah."

She let out a long sigh and tapped on the contact list, slowly she typed "Dad". Her fingers lingered over the number, which was imprinted in her memory, but an unseen force was pulling her away from tapping the name. After several minutes of contemplation, she opened up WhatsApp and found her dad's name parked at the top of the list.

"Happy Birthday Dad," she typed out hesitantly. Just when she was about to hit send, she saw her dad typing…

'Would have loved to hear your voice today.'

She felt her heart sink. She knew she needed to call him, but the possibility of the uncomfortable silence made her hesitant. "I will call you in some time, promise, Happy Birthday!" she typed back and quickly closed the app.

Her phone buzzed again, and she noticed the innumerable notifications. While she scrolled through the notifications, her thumb froze over Google Memories. She tapped on the notification, and an ambient melody began to play as memories from the past emerged in the form of images on her phone.

Mountains; her dad cutting a cake; her brother smearing cake on her face; her mother and father side hugging while smiling awkwardly into the camera; large gatherings of smartly dressed uncles and aunties laughing in a garden.

Scrolling through the images, her heart felt heavy with nostalgia. She stopped at a family photo from when she was 14 years old. They were all standing in front of each other, bending at strange angles to make sure their cake-smeared faces were fully visible. While reminiscing about that day, she couldn't help but smile at the genuine joy on her teenage face, a rare sight at that age. However, her happiness wasn't just because of her father's birthday celebration. The best return gift he could have given her was allowing her to depart for boarding school the very next day. It was a relief after years of relocating due to her father's army duties. Finally, she was hopeful of finding a sense of rootedness. It was at the boarding school where she met her best friends, Mehul and Anshika. For the first time in a long time, she felt like she was at home.

The comforting aroma of ginger and lemon wafted from her cup of hot tea, yet it failed to ease her grumpiness. Aaliyah despised it when her routine was disrupted without her consent. While she cherished her weekend mornings sleeping in, her dear friends often spoiled them with drunken calls, a punishment she accepted for occasionally needing her solitude.

After a heavy lunch, she lounged on her sofa and lazily scrolled through the endless list of content suggestions on her television. While scrolling through the options, her thumb paused when her eyes noticed an interesting title on the screen.

"The Nature of Ayahuasca"

Gazing at the screen, her eyes fixed on the title and description before her. The word "Ayahuasca" leapt out, tugging at her with an inexplicable force. A peculiar thrill surged through her as she contemplated the prospect of finally experiencing this mystical psychedelic brew after years of ruminating on it since her college days, back when she had first heard of it. Five long years had passed, and yet the allure of Ayahuasca had only grown stronger within her.

"Don't be silly Aaliyah, it's never gonna happen" said the voice inside and she continued to scroll.

While Family Guy played softly in the background, she found herself gradually drifting off into a peaceful doze. Suddenly, a loud bang on her door startled her awake. She sprang up from the sofa and cautiously made her way towards the peephole to see who was there. It turned out to be Mehul, who always seemed to ruin her peaceful weekends.

She opened the door and asked, "You know I have a doorbell, right?"

Mehul sheepishly grinned and replied, "Yes, but this was more fun."

"You're such an idiot," she smirked, slapping the back of his head playfully as he barged into her house. Mehul plonked himself on the sofa and grabbed the remote to scroll through the list. After a few minutes of surfing, he turned to Aaliyah, "So, did you do any research for the trip?"

"What trip?", she responded with a slight smirk

Mehul let out an exasperated sigh and exclaimed, "I thought I was the one with a terrible hangover. Amazon, hello!"

"Is that really happening?" She inquired playfully.

"Of course, it's happening, what do you mean?" he replied, with a hint of irritation in his voice.

"I thought it would be one of *those* plans,"

"Liya, this trip is happening! And it needs to happen soon, so don't waste any time," he insisted, his tone determined. Aaliyah groaned, her frustration evident.

"Stop being such a couch potato. You were so spontaneous when we were in college, why have you become so boring these days?" he teased, a mischievous glint in his eyes.

"I'm just being practical, Mehul. It's not like we are planning a trip to Goa. And unlike you, we work for other people, and getting an extended holiday on such short notice may not happen," she retorted, her voice laced with a hint of annoyance and logic.

"Did you even ask her?" He prodded, "You're giving up without a fight. That dickhead Kartik really messed you up, Liya."

She winced at Mehul's words. Several years ago, the mere mention of that name would have sparked an effervescent smile on her face. However, in the last two years, every time she stumbled upon that name, it felt as though a merciless assailant was relentlessly plunging a searing hot branding iron into her heart, causing an excruciating pain that refused to dissipate. They spent three years together and even moved in with each other, but everything came crashing down when she found out about his infidelity. To make matters worse, the person he had cheated on her with was her own flatmate and close friend of three years. The betrayal left her feeling devastated and alone.

She rolled her eyes and let out a sigh. "Please, could you try to not ruin my weekend any further?"

Mehul quickly apologised, "Sorry, my bad." Then, in an effort to diffuse the tension, he asked, "Hey, do we have any lemon fizz in the fridge?"

She responded dryly, "Go see for yourself."

"I was checking earlier," Mehul continued, undeterred, "September is the best time to go."

"That's not too far away."

"Exactly!" Mehul exclaimed with enthusiasm.

"Ok ok, let's see"

"That's the spirit! Trust me, you'll thank me when we are there. Maybe when you see all the beautiful Brazilian women, you'll realise that you're actually interested in the chicas."

"I think I would know by now," she said, smirking at him.

Reluctantly, she got out of the diwan and grabbed her laptop to get into her beloved planner mode. The rest of the day went by in heated discussions and laughter as they scrolled through websites, learning more about the biggest rainforest in the world.

Even though she gave in to the plan in front of Mehul, she wasn't too convinced that this would happen. She secretly hoped that someone would bail in her friend circle, and she wouldn't have to look like the killjoy.

The following days went by pretty rapidly. To Aaliyah's surprise and dismay, everything seemed to be falling into place, and the plan to go to the Amazon was materialising in front of her eyes. Hoping that her boss would reject her leave application, she was shocked when her boss was happy that she was finally utilising her holidays and even offered to help get good deals in Brazil for their stay. Aaliyah felt like the Amazons were almost pulling them in, and she started getting a bit concerned about how smoothly everything was working out.

One evening, when Mehul was visiting her after work, she shared her concern. "*Yaar*, I am not used to such smooth plans, I feel something will go wrong when we're there."

"*Chup re*, don't overthink."

"I'm serious, Mehul. I'd prefer if something went wrong now because then I'd know the trip would go well."

"Well, what's the worst that can happen? Our plane could crash, we could contract some incurable disease, or one of us could die. That's it."

"Is that supposed to be funny?" she asked with a straight face.

"*Arre*, after hearing this, you'll flip out even more."

She looked at him, concerned.

"You remember my friend Daniel from Brazil? He's in India right now. He called this morning and asked if he could bunk at my place for a couple of nights before he flies back home. I told him about our plan, and he basically invited himself. So now he's extending his stay so he can travel with us."

She stared at him wide-eyed.

"AND he's offered to host us at his ancestral home in Sao Luiz so we don't need to worry about our stay and he will take us around. So now our stay is sorted, and we have a local guide."

"Lucky us!" she said sarcastically.

"Indeed!"

"The best part about all this is that he knows some authentic places where we can do Ayahuasca because he's done it before."

Her face lit up. "That's actually great!"

"Finally, some genuine excitement," smirked Mehul.

During a backpacking trip, Kartik introduced Aaliyah to Ayahuasca. They bonded over their shared interest and made grand plans to experience the magical drink together in the Amazons. This instant connection during their first encounter made her believe that Kartik would be her backpacking partner for life. However, this dream was short-lived because soon she discovered that he preferred the fast-paced city life filled with parties and bar-hopping- activities that didn't align with her interests. Despite their differences, she clung to their relationship, hoping to find the stability and security that had been missing from her life.

While musing on this, she muttered something in Portuguese.

"Nice job, dude, sounds like we're getting better at it. Will you know enough to flirt with the Brazilian chicas?"

"Sure," she said, rolling her eyes.

In the days that followed, there was a lot of excitement and drama, which annoyed Aaliyah because she hated drama. However, as the official planner, she had no choice.

* * *

After six long weeks of meticulous planning and anticipation, they finally arrived at their destination. Excitement rippled through Aaliyah and her five friends as they descended the escalator and stepped into the bustling Sao Luiz International Airport. The vast space was filled with the sounds of chatter and the bustle of travellers, creating a palpable sense of energy that swept through the group.

The journey to Brazil had been gruelling, lasting twenty-two hours, but the group was buoyed by the thrill of discovery that awaited them. As they made their way through the airport, their excitement grew with each passing moment, their hearts pounding with anticipation for what lay beyond.

"Did you see the forest?" Gauri screamed at Aaliyah

"I did!" Aaliyah responded with mild excitement.

Mehul sensed Aaliyah's annoyance with Gauri and grabbed her hand. "Come babe, I want some selfies with you before we get to immigration."

"YESS!!" Gauri screamed and walked away with Mehul.

After a tedious immigration process, the group finally emerged from the airport and were greeted by a blast of humid air.

"Oh Lord, my hair is gonna be screwed," complained Anshika.

"I warned you, you should've just shaved your head for the trip," said Mehul mockingly.

"Who asked you?" Anshika retorted while tying her frizzy brown hair into a tight bun.

"Children, let's not begin our trip with a fight, okay?" Aaliyah said while placing her hands on both their shoulders.

"Guys, look for a short, balding, middle-aged man," Daniel announced to everyone.

"There's your man, Mr Denial!" exclaimed Mehul, gesturing towards a stout man displaying a large sign with the words 'Mr Denial' scrawled across it.

"Oh haha! Carlos is like family, he has been taking care of our ancestral home for 30 years now."

"Oh, wow!" exclaimed Gauri.

Daniel hugged Carlos and introduced him to everyone.

"How long will it take to get to your place?" Gauri inquired enthusiastically.

"About an hour," Daniel responded as he threw his backpack in the trunk of the Range Rover.

"Oh well, what's another hour of sitting after 22?" Anshika mumbled while scooting into the back seat.

"Why so crabby, Ansh? You can sleep the rest of the day," comforted Aaliyah.

"Yo! We didn't come all the way to sleep, grams, tonight we're going out!" Mehul intervened.

"Ok, ok, we'll see. Now get in." Aaliyah responded quickly.

"Okay everyone, keep a close eye on your wallets and purses, now *Vamos*!" Daniel reminded the group, his voice laced with a hint of urgency, before firmly shutting the car door behind him. The friends scrambled to load themselves into the vehicle, their hearts racing with a mix of excitement and apprehension. Once they settled into their seats, they took a moment to look around and soak in their surroundings. The car was spacious and comfortable, with plush leather seats and cool air conditioning that offered a welcome respite from the hot and humid climate outside.

As Carlos pulled away from the curb, the group gazed out the windows, taking in the sights and sounds of the bustling city. The streets were lined with vendors hawking their wares, and the air was thick with the scent of exotic spices and cooked food. The cacophony of honking horns and the buzz of activity added to the frenzied energy. Despite the flurry of activity around them, the friends couldn't help but feel a sense of exhilaration and wonder at the adventure that lay ahead.

Medicine

"I might have to shave my head before we leave this place," complained Anshika while struggling to untangle her frizzy mane.

"You shouldn't have grown your hair, Ansh. Long hair isn't your thing," commented Aaliyah while tying her shoes.

"Thanks, that's not helpful at all," rebuked Anshika while struggling to pull out the hairbrush stuck in her hair.

"I hope that idiot Mehul doesn't piss me off today." She said while tying her hair in an untidy bun.

"Haha, I'll be sure to keep my camera ready to capture those precious moments! Ready to go?" asked Aaliyah, as she stood up and grabbed her pouch.

"Yeah, let's check if the idiot wants to come along," Anshika responded while walking out the door. They headed towards the neighbouring cottage where Mehul and Gauri were staying. After their third knock went unanswered, they gave up and decided to explore the retreat on their own.

Anshika's voice quivered with a mixture of disbelief and excitement as they strolled towards the deck that overlooked the lush garden.

"Can you believe that we're actually standing in the Amazon?" she exclaimed in amazement. Overcome with emotion, she grabbed Aaliyah by the arm and pulled her into a tight hug. They sank down onto the wooden stairs, staring out at the breathtaking scene before them. The enormity of the garden and the lush jungle beyond it left them both speechless.

The garden was a masterpiece of nature, with towering trees that seemed to reach up to the sky, their leaves rustling gently in the breeze. The duo gazed in awe at the dense jungle beyond the garden, filled with lush greenery and exotic flora. The verdant garden was a riot of colour, with sprawling plants and vines that intertwined with each other, creating a tapestry of green and red. The scarlet lobster-claws were a sight to behold, with their bright, vivid blooms that seemed to glow in the dappled sunlight. The rich purple orchids added another layer of beauty to the garden, with their delicate petals and intricate designs. They sat there, surrounded by the fragrant aroma of the forest, the gentle coolness of the earth beneath them, and the soothing warmth of the breeze on their skin. The sound of birds and insects filled the air, making it feel like they were in another world.

Anshika turned to Aaliyah and said, "Look at the frogs jumping into the lily pond. Such cuties!" Aaliyah turned her gaze to the pond, watching as the bright creatures hopped from one lily pad to another, their bright yellow skin shimmering in the sunlight.

"This place is surreal," she said, "I feel like we're in a dream."

Transfixed with the beauty of the jungle, Anshika murmured, "I'm so glad we're doing this,"

Aaliyah rolled her eyes and responded sarcastically, "I can't believe we actually made a drunken plan happen."

Anshika turned to Aaliyah with a warm smile, "I'm really glad that you made this happen, thank you."

"We should do this more often, I really miss spending time with you," said Aaliyah with her voice cracking.

Anshika nodded, "I know life gets busy, but you have to make time for what really matters."

Aaliyah sighed, "You're right, but it's not always easy. Work takes up so much of my time."

"Don't lct work consume you Liya," Anshika advised, "You can always make time for the people you care about."

"You're right," Aaliyah smiled gently

Anshika pulled her in for another hug, "Okay, now let's go."

En route to the temple, they paused every few steps, unable to resist admiring the breathtaking scenery that surrounded them. The trees towered over them, their branches creating a canopy overhead. The sunlight filtered through the leaves, dappling the forest floor with patches of light and shadow. The duo walked slowly, taking in every detail of the natural beauty around them.

Anshika hopped over the small bridge over the lily pond and asked, "Have you thought about tonight's ceremony and what you want to address during the session?"

"Sort of, but I need to pen it down. Did you think of your points?" asked Aaliyah.

"Not yet, I was hoping to keep it open-ended. I'm pretty messed up overall." sneered Anshika

"That you are, but I suggest you think about something more specific. Don't think you'll get fully fixed in one session anyway." laughed Aaliyah.

"You're right! Tackle one devil at a time."

Aaliyah had been researching Ayahuasca for many years and was pretty clear on the areas of her life that she wanted to resolve. She had been reflecting on her internal demons and was certain that Ayahuasca would help her resolve those issues.

They made their way towards the temple, their footsteps crunching on the fallen leaves that littered the grassy ground. The temple was nestled amongst the towering trees, and it seemed to grow out of the very earth itself. It was a circular building made entirely of bamboo, with slender bamboo pillars that reached towards the sky. The roof was tall and thatched, providing shade from the bright sun and shelter from the rain.

Drawing closer, they could see that the vines that had grown up the pillars of the temple and intertwined themselves into a natural lattice, creating a stunning organic pattern. The vines were thick and green, with leaves as big as dinner plates that filtered the light that shone through them.

Approaching the entrance, they were greeted by a simple yet charming wooden gate, adorned with a flurry of colourful flowers and twisting vines that seemed to stretch towards the sky. The gate stood ajar, beckoning them inside with an air of friendly invitation. Upon stepping into the temple, they were immediately struck by the serene beauty of the space. The interior was both spacious and breezy, with enormous open windows that flooded the room with light and allowed the fresh scent of the jungle to waft in. The walls were made of woven bamboo, creating a delicate lattice pattern that allowed them to look out into the jungle. In the heart of the temple, a small altar was adorned with an array of blooming flowers and flickering candles. The elegant simplicity of the space created a peaceful, reflective atmosphere that felt perfectly attuned to the ceremony they had come to participate in.

They looked around for Juan, the shaman's assistant they had met the previous evening, but he was nowhere to be seen. Suddenly, from behind the door of a small room adjacent to the temple hall, they heard an angelic voice chanting a beautiful melody. Intrigued, they stepped out of the temple and followed the ethereal voice, which led them to the back of the temple. There, smoke filled the air, accompanied by a strong woody scent mixed with hints of vinegar.

Approaching closer, they spotted Mama Alandra, the shaman, alongside her husband Jorge, their daughter Maria, and Juan gathered around a modest fire pit. It was Mama Alandra who had been the source of the otherworldly melody from within the temple. She sat next to a large iron pot situated atop a wood fire, from which steam wafted out, while Jorge intermittently stirred the contents with a large wooden ladle. The pot contained dark orange-brown vines and vibrant green leaves submerged in water, slowly boiling and releasing their earthy aroma. A bunch of vines and leaves were placed in separate containers on the ground next to the pot. Juan and Maria were engaged in the task of separating and pounding the vines, meticulously removing stems and bugs from the leaves, before finally transferring them to a spacious aluminium container.

Upon spotting their approach, Juan extended an invitation for them to observe the preparation of the medicine. Grateful for the opportunity, they accepted and settled beside Mama Alandra and Jorge. Anshika leaned towards Juan and inquired in a hushed tone, "What is Mama Alandra singing?"

Juan replied in a similarly soft voice, "She is singing the sacred *icaros*. It is a song meant to invoke the blessings of the spirits and ancestors upon the ayahuasca potion and the ceremony."

"What plants do you use to make the Ayahuasca?" Aaliyah asked Juan, pointing at the stems and leaves in the holy potion.

"The orange stem is from the ayahuasca plant, and the leaves are from the Chacruna plant. We boil them together to make the medicine."

"Can I feel the effects if I chew on these leaves?" asked Anshika, picking up some leaves from the ground.

Juan laughed, "No, no, it is very bitter, you will puke before it can have any effect. When we boil these together, they make a strong soup of the plant juices that help in the therapy."

"Can we take these to India?" asked Anshika.

"No no, a lot of checking happens at the airport. And it is not safe to have this medicine without the guidance of a trained shaman."

"I was joking, we won't take it,"

While they were intently looking at the brewing procedure, a pair of blue and black butterflies flitted close to the ayahuasca vines kept on the ground and floated away back towards the forest after a few moments."Oh wow!" gasped Anshika

"*Ancestrais estão abençoando a cerimônia*'" said Mama Alandra, smiling.

The girls turn to Juan inquisitively. "She is saying that the ancestors are blessing the ceremony. Butterflies are considered to be a symbol of *transformação.*"

"Transformation," Aaliyah mumbled to Anshika.

Aaliyah attempted to converse in her limited Portuguese, asking about the ceremony and Mama Alandra's experience with Ayahuasca. The shaman explained that her family had been practising the tradition for over four generations and she was now training her own children to continue the legacy.

"Where will you go after your stay here?" asked Juan.

"*Estamos planejando acampar na floresta por alguns dias,*"Aaliyah responded in her broken Portuguese.

"*não!*" The shaman almost screamed at them and furiously waved her hand, signalling them not to go.

"*por que não?*" Aaliyah inquired meekly.

"*Perigo, perigo,*" the shaman mumbled nervously and walked away.

Startled by the shaman's reaction to their further plans, they turned to Juan, seeking reassurance. Ignoring what he had just heard, he kept his attention on preparing the vines. Observing his lack of response, the girls inferred that it was time to depart and stood up. Aaliyah thanked them for their hospitality, and they walked back toward the cottages. After walking a significant distance away from where they could be overheard, Anshika asked, "What on earth was that all about?"

"I have no idea. She reacted as if I threatened to kill her," said Aaliyah with a slight smirk.

"But what did you say to her?" Anshika asked impatiently.

"I just told them that we are planning to camp in the forest for a few days."

"Oh! And what does *perigo* mean?" Asked Anshika nervously.

"Danger," Aaliyah said in an irritable voice.

"That's not encouraging. Should we cancel our plan? I mean, she wouldn't react like that if there wasn't something really dangerous out there, right?" Anshika inquired, anxiety dripping from her words.

"Relax Ansh, maybe she didn't understand what I was saying. We'll talk to Daniel,"

As they walked back towards the cottages, they spot Daniel in the garden practising yoga with some other guests. Noticing their approach, he walked towards them.

"Mornin' girls! Where are you coming from?"

"We just went to explore the place and then sat with Mama Alandra and her family, watching them prepare the brew for tonight," Aaliyah responded.

"Brilliant! Excited for the evening?" he chirped.

"Yes of course! But something weird happened right now. When we mentioned that we were planning to camp in the forest for a few days she lost it and started screaming 'danger, danger' and just walked away. I couldn't even ask her anything else. Do you think we should reconsider going into the forest? Or do you want to ask some locals about this?"

"First of all, I AM a local! And don't worry about it. People here usually discourage tourists because most people can't handle the forest. But I've camped in the forest many times. It's not threatening in any way," he boasted.

"Um, okay," she replied with a hint of unease in her voice. "We're gonna go back to the cottage and see what the others are doing," she added, motioning Anshika to leave.

"Alright, I'll see you, ladies, around," he said while walking back towards his yoga mat.

Anshika's voice was barely audible as they walked away from Daniel. "I don't feel very confident with his response,"

Aaliyah nodded in agreement, her own voice hesitant. "Hmmm, same here. But he's a local, so I guess we should trust him."

As those words left her mouth, Aaliyah's heart sank. The knot of anxiety in her chest tightened, and she struggled to maintain her composure. She tried to focus on the delicate white flowers along the path back to the cottages, but the shaman's warning rang loudly in her ears. Though she was hesitant to ignore the warning, she didn't want to ruin their plans after coming such a long way.

Anshika looked at her with concern. "Are you okay, Liya?"

She forced a smile, but her eyes betrayed her fear. "I'm fine."

On their way back, they bump into Rehaan. "Hey hey! Good morning. Where were you, ladies?"

"We just went exploring the place. They are brewing the Ayahuasca at the temple."

"Neat! I'll go check that out. I need to shoot some content for my channel. See you later," he said as he hopped towards the temple.

Aaliyah and Anshika made their way towards the deck, only to find Mehul standing shirtless by their door, leaning against the wooden railing. He was completely engrossed in taking photographs of a gargantuan centipede that precariously perched on a small branch of a nearby tree.

"Morning, Lazy!" Anshika screamed in his ears.

"Annshh, I was going to drop my phone, you idiot," he said irritably, keeping his phone in his pocket.

"Why didn't you open the door in the morning? We knocked a hundred times. I hope you weren't getting it on," Aaliyah said winking at him.

"No, dude. Gauri wasn't feeling too well last evening when we went to the room. She had a slight temperature, but she's better now."

"Oh, no. Is she OK to have Ayahuasca tonight?"

"I think so. She woke up super excited this morning, but I asked her to get more rest so she's ready for the evening."

"Wow! You are capable of being smart sometimes." Mocked Aaliyah. Mehul smirked at her as he pushed her towards the centipede that was inching closer to the railing. "Urgh spoke too soon," she said, shaking her head.

"We saw them brewing the drink at the temple!" Anshika announced.

"Killer! Did you get some photographs?"

"Nah, Mr. Youtube has gone to capture the process. So don't worry about the documentation. Although, while we were there, the shaman warned us from going to the forest. But we spoke to Daniel and he said that there's nothing to worry about,"

"Hmm, yeah man don't think about it. He's from here. I'm sure we'll be fine."

With the sun beginning its descent, a soft drumming sound, reminiscent of the heartbeat of the earth, could be heard in the distance. The six friends, eagerly waiting in Daniel's room for the ceremony to begin, jumped to their feet, grabbed their belongings, and made their way to the temple.

The mystical sounds of the *icaros* welcomed them with open arms as they approached. The music danced through the air, creating a symphony of rhythm and harmony. The friends entered the large circular temple, where a dimly lit ambience was set by the gentle evening glow of the sun seeping in through the large windows. The atmosphere was warm and inviting, and the room was adorned with feathers, flowers, and vines from the forest, casually hanging from the walls. Single mattresses with multi-coloured bedspreads were placed neatly around the room, inviting the guests to lay down and soak in the sacred energy of the space. The soft, inviting glow and melodic sounds created a serene and tranquil environment, a place where the soul could be nourished and the spirit could soar.

"Wow! This is gorgeous!" Gauri whispered excitedly as they made their way towards the mattresses.

In the centre of the room, Mama Alandra sat regally, eyes closed, draped in colourful traditional garments, adorned with an array of feathers delicately interwoven into her hair. The sweet scent of copal incense filled the air, mingling with the rich, musky aroma of tobacco smoke emanating from Jorge, who sat beside Mama Alandra in a trance-like state. With her angelic voice, Mama Alandra sang the sacred *icaros*, her voice weaving a magical spell around the room. The sound echoed off the walls and reverberated through the space, filling it with a sense of otherworldliness.

Juan, who sat against the wall a few feet behind the couple, rose gracefully to light the candles as the guests found their designated mattresses, scattered about the room.

With the guests settling in, Juan's drumming filled the room with a subtle bass, providing a steady heartbeat that anchored the ceremony. The *icaros* continued, weaving a tapestry of sound that swirled around the room, leaving the guests mesmerised. Mama Alandra's voice rose and fell, like a bird in flight, carrying the guests on a journey of the soul. Her voice filled the space, and the energy in the room was palpable as if the very air was charged with magic. After almost an hour, Mama Alandra stopped singing, and the room was filled with a hushed silence. Juan took this as his cue to begin the ceremony, and the guests sat in rapt attention, eagerly awaiting for what was to come.

"Good evening, friends. We welcome you to the holy temple of Mother Aya. Tonight you will experience Mother Aya's grace as you drink the holy medicine. We will offer you one glass of the holy medicine. After drinking, you will need to wait for 30-60 minutes to start feeling the effects. Before we begin giving you the holy medicine, please take 10 minutes to write down the questions you want answers for during this experience." Before Juan could finish speaking, most of the participants raised small pieces of paper, on which their questions were written.

"Okay good. Looks like we are all well prepared! When the medicine starts working, you will feel a need to purge, either through puking, crying, or going to the toilet. This purging is important, as your body throws away the physical and emotional rubbish that you have collected in your life. There is a bucket next to each of your beds, use that for puking, and the toilets are right outside the temple. After drinking the medicine, you should lie on the bed and allow Mother Aya to come to you. Trust in her power and guidance, and she will show you the light."

After instructing the eager participants, Juan gestured to Daniel, who was seated closest to him, to approach Mama Alandra to receive the medicine.

Each participant, one after the other, made their way to the centre of the room and sat before Mama Alandra and her husband. The husband blew wafts of thick smoke and filled the room with its musky fragrance, while Mama Alandra poured a small amount of the medicine into a mud tumbler, offering it to each participant.

After the first five people had consumed the medicine, it was Aaliyah's turn. She sat before the shaman, and with trembling hands, she accepted the tumbler of dark liquid from the shaman. She looked up at the shaman and her anxious gaze met the wise woman's droopy, calm eyes, providing her with a sense of reassurance and safety. Aaliyah stared down at the drink for a moment, and then she heard the shaman's voice, *"confie na mãe aya."*

Aaliyah looked up at her and gave her a warm smile. Mama Alandra returned the smile, nodding her head. With a deep breath, she raised the mud tumbler to her lips and swallowed the medicine in one gulp. Almost immediately, she felt an intense urge to vomit. She quickly covered her mouth with her hand, determined to keep the medicine down. She turned to Mama Alandra and thanked her for the medicine, then made her way back to her mattress, where Mehul was waiting anxiously. He gestured to her, asking if she was okay, and

Aaliyah responded with a reassuring thumbs-up, settling down onto her mattress.

"How does it taste?" Anshika asked, standing up and ready for her turn.

"You'll find out soon," she responded with a grimace, causing the group to chuckle in anticipation.

Aaliyah sank into her comfortable mattress, quietly observing as the rest of the participants took their turns drinking the thick, murky medicine. Once everyone had been offered the sacred drink, the shaman and her husband swallowed their own doses and resumed singing the *icaros*. The husband exhaled plumes of smoke that curled and twisted in the air, casting ethereal shadows on the walls, as their hauntingly beautiful voices continued to fill the dimly lit temple.

Within 30 minutes, people began to hurl into their buckets as the medicine started to take effect. Aaliyah, on the other hand, was still waiting for the sensation to hit her. She looked around the room and noticed Mehul lying on his back with his eyes closed, and Anshika had been absent for over 10 minutes, likely in the bathroom. Panic set in for her, wondering why the medicine wasn't working on her. She fidgeted with the edge of her bedspread and considered approaching Mama Alandra for another shot. However, just as she was about to get up to request it, she was overcome with sudden and overwhelming drowsiness. It felt as though an invisible force was pressing down on her, trapping her in her spot. Giving in, she sank into the mattress and closed her eyes. Laying on the soft mattress, she felt herself slipping away into a dark, infinite void, and the sound of the *icaros* started fading into silence.

She heard a voice whisper in her ear, "Trust Mother Aya."

Mama Aya

Aaliyah clenched the bedsheet as she felt the heavy weight pressing down on her chest, sinking her deeper into the soft mattress. She squirmed in discomfort, feeling the heat of the medicine spreading rapidly through her body. A burning sensation surged within her like a raging river, eliciting a sense of panic that flowed through her veins. The heat inside felt like strings of fire writhing throughout her body. Her panic escalated dangerously until the rhythm of the *icaros* shifted, causing the energy in the room to transform. Slowly, her hands relaxed as the once-black abyss surrounding her began to glow, revealing a mesmerizing kaleidoscope of vibrant, brilliant colours she had never witnessed before. Gradually, the intense heat within her body subsided, and she found herself captivated by the enchanting dance of lights encircling her.

Struggling to comprehend the breathtaking spectacle before her, the light tunnel gradually moved towards a dark wall. She tried to resist the pull of the darkness, but something urged her to trust the fall. Giving in to the void, she plunged into the inky blackness. Once again, panic gripped her, and she struggled to regain her bearings by searching for any sign of her surroundings. Unable to see, she felt her body submerged in a liquid, the weight of it pressing down on her waist while the top of her body felt weightless. She flailed around in confusion, trying to make sense of the sensation. She tried to walk around but found herself stuck in one place. She waved her hand around and tried to hold onto something when she felt the liquid pulling her down. The realization that she could be sinking into a swamp caused panic to rise within her again. Frantically, she tried to look for solid ground and threw her hands around to grab something.

After some struggle, she was able to latch onto what felt like an arm. Straining to discern what she had caught, her gaze sharpened, and a feminine silhouette emerged, gradually transforming from a sombre midnight blue to a luminous and radiant white. She felt blinded by the glow of this beautiful feminine figure. "Mama Aya," whispered the gentle breeze. She stopped struggling and surrendered to Mama Aya, allowing her to lead her on the journey. Effortlessly, she pulled Aaliyah out of the water and onto solid ground, illuminating the surroundings as she glided ahead.

She continued to gaze at the back of Mama Aya's head, where she could see beautiful white tresses that fell over her soft white shoulders like feathers. She tried to see her face, but Mama Aya was focused on the path ahead.

Following Mama Aya through the clearing, the colours surrounding her transformed into a dazzling display. The sky above was initially a deep blue, nearly indigo, but as she progressed further, it gradually lightened and brightened into a vivid cerulean shade. The trees around them were twisted and gnarled, their branches reaching out like bony fingers towards the sky. The leaves on the trees were a bright, neon green that seemed to pulse and throb with energy. Walking along, Aaliyah became aware of a low humming sound resonating from the earth beneath her feet. It was a strange, otherworldly noise, and it made the hairs on the back of her neck stand up. Despite her fear, however, she felt a deep sense of calm and peace emanating from Mama Aya. She knew she was safe with her.

Gliding deeper into the forest, she noticed strange creatures darting in and out of the trees. These creatures were unlike anything she had ever seen before; some were brightly coloured and winged, while others were furry and moved with a strange, loping gait. As they drew closer, the creatures seemed to shy away from them, as if they were afraid of Mama Aya.

After what felt like hours of walking, they emerged into a small clearing. In the centre of the clearing was a large, shimmering pool of water. Through the crystal-clear water, strange, glowing shapes could be seen moving beneath the surface. Aaliyah felt the urge to dive in and join them, but Mama Aya held her back.

"Not yet," she said, her voice echoing through the clearing like a bell. "We have much more to see."

With that, they moved on, deeper into the forest. Aaliyah was filled with a sense of wonder and awe as she followed Mama Aya. She didn't know where they were going or what they would see next, but she knew that she was in the hands of a powerful and ancient force and that wherever they went, she would be safe.

While she struggled to understand her surroundings, Mama Aya's grasp slipped away from her gradually. Watching the luminous figure drift further and further away, a sense of despair overtook her. Desperate to catch up with it, she took hurried steps, but in her haste, she stumbled over the uneven ground and fell to her knees. As she regained her balance, she heard familiar voices. Straining to listen, she recognized her parents' distinct tones: her father's deep baritone and her mother's soft but assertive voice.

She scanned the area for the source of the sounds and saw a holographic projection of her parents engaged in a heated argument, while her younger self and brother watched from the sidelines. Her heart sank as she remembered the time when her parents were considering separation due to the challenges of balancing their careers and raising their children. Her mother wanted to move back to Aaliyah's grandparents' house for support, but her father was against the idea. The argument seemed to be reaching a boiling point with the words 'separation,' 'kids,' and 'career' being thrown around.

While she was processing the memory, she noticed that Mama Aya had moved farther away and was drifting through the darkness, illuminating her path. Determined to follow her, she set out towards the glowing figure. However, she was stopped in her tracks by a loud scream that sounded like her brother. She turned to see another holographic projection, this time of her parents trying to console her inconsolable brother, who was crying and demanding not to be separated from his sister. Watching the scene as an observer, she realised that her parents were struggling just as much as the children to find a solution. Feeling sympathy for them, she observed how the demands of a young child had left them defeated.

When she turned back to Mama Aya, she witnessed the luminous figure gradually fading away into what seemed to be the edge of a forest. She quickened her pace, hoping to catch up to the spiritual being when she heard a deep voice that sent shivers down her spine. Turning to her side, she saw herself and Kartik engaged in a heated argument. This was during the time when they were living together and she wanted to go on a trip for her birthday, but Kartik wanted to stay back due to work deadlines. Watching the argument, she realized the insignificance of their disagreement in the grand scheme of things. Observing the fight as an outsider, she realized that the argument was unnecessary and that she might have overreacted at the time. Shaking her head, she felt slightly embarrassed about her past behaviour. She knew that the past couldn't be changed, but she could learn from it.

Making her way through the darkness, she found herself looking at another argument between herself and Kartik. She stood there watching, as they argued heatedly about house chores. Both refusing to take responsibility, blaming each other for not doing their part. However, Aaliyah's keen eyes and ears revealed that the real problem was deeper than just household chores. The frustration in their voices was not about the house duties, but a lack of trust and dependability between them.

Listening to their raised voices, she couldn't help but feel a sense of déjà vu. It was like watching a scene from her parents' marriage play out before her. The same words, the same tone, the same emotions. She could feel her heart sinking with a heavy weight of realisation. She had always thought that she and Kartik had a different kind of relationship, but now she was able to see the truth. They were repeating the same patterns of her parent's marriage, and it was terrifying. Aaliyah wanted to scream, to make them see what they were doing to each other, but her voice was stuck in her throat. She could only stand there, watching helplessly as their argument continued. She observed the unpleasant engagement for some more time and felt a little less hatred toward Kartik. She realised that he was not the only one responsible for their failed relationship. Her life would have been much simpler if only she clearly communicated what she felt inside.

While musing on her past, she could sense the light dimming from the corner of her eyes. She realised that Mama Aya was now disappearing into the darkness, and she knew that she had to act fast if she wanted to follow her. She decided not to get distracted by the voices any more, which continued to prop from every direction and decided to sprint towards Mama Aya. She ran past many holographic images of different times in her life, some happy and some sad. She saw herself as a child, playing with her brother in the park. She saw precious moments spent with her friends at a party. She saw herself as a young adult, struggling to make ends meet. She saw all the ups and downs of her life, and she knew that they had made her who she was today.

Running, her heart pounded in her chest, and her breaths came in short gasps. Despite this, she didn't stop. She kept on until she finally reached Mama Aya, now resembling a tall blue flame. Approaching closer, she touched the flame, which dissipated like smoke, and she found herself looking at a beautiful clearing with a large blue lake. The lake was surrounded by trees, and the water was crystal clear. She could see fish swimming in the lake and birds flying overhead. The air was fresh and smelled of jasmine and lemongrass.

While strolling towards the lake, she couldn't help but be mesmerised by the tranquil glow emanating from the pristine waters. The towering trees surrounding the lake were adorned with the most vibrant leaves that seemed to be alive with the hues of the rainbow. As she tilted her head back, her eyes were drawn to the sky's mesmerizing tapestry. Countless stars adorned the vast darkness, their brilliance flickering and painting the expanse with a celestial palette. Each twinkle seemed to whisper secrets of the universe, evoking a profound sense of awe that stirred her soul. A lump formed in her throat, stifling words that could not capture the depth of her emotions.

Compelled by the cosmic display, she inched towards the tranquil lake. A soft glow emanated from beneath the water's surface, casting a gentle radiance that beckoned her closer. Step by step, anticipation coursed through her veins as she approached the mystical source.

As the glow intensified, a figure emerged from the depths, gradually ascending with graceful movements. Bathed in iridescent light, it possessed an otherworldly beauty that defied her understanding. Was it a mortal being, blessed with extraordinary allure, or some ethereal creature from realms beyond her comprehension? The answer eluded her, leaving her in a state of wonder and enchantment.

She moved in for a closer look but accidentally stepped into the lake. She peered down into the surface of the water and saw a dark figure staring back at her. She gasped and took a few steps back, her grip on the lake bed slipping. When she looked up again, she found herself standing where the ethereal figure once stood. She looked down and saw the murky figure looking back at her, sending shivers down her spine. Closing her eyes, she turned away as tears began to stream down her face. Her weeping grew louder and more intense, and it seemed like a cathartic release of all the pent-up emotions she had been carrying for far too long. Her sobs echoed through the surrounding trees as she let out all the pain and fear that had been holding her back.

Tears streamed down Aaliyah's face, tracing paths of raw emotion. In that vulnerable moment, a gentle touch landed on her forehead, drawing her attention. She opened her eyes to find Mama Alandra crouched beside her, wearing a tender smile that radiated warmth and kindness. Their gazes met, and Aaliyah sensed a profound understanding that transcended words. The floodgates of her anguish burst open, and she surrendered to her tears, allowing the catharsis to wash over her. Time lost meaning as she wept, feeling as though the sorrow would never wane.

After what felt like an eternity, the tears gradually receded, leaving behind a respite in their wake. The compassionate shaman, blew a thick puff of tobacco smoke that enveloped Aaliyah, infusing the air with a sweet and calming aroma. The tendrils of smoke swirled around her, cocooning her in a serene embrace. As Mama Alandra resumed singing the icaros, Aaliyah sensed a gentle, encompassing warmth seeping into her being, restoring her equilibrium. Rising to her feet, the shaman returned to the centre of the temple leaving Aaliyah to ponder the beauty and enigma of the lake.

Her heart rate slowed down, and her breathing returned to normal as she regained her composure. She became acutely aware of her surroundings and began to take in the details of the temple. Upon scanning the room, she noticed that some of the other participants were missing from their beds, while others still lay motionless. Her attention was drawn towards Anshika's bed, but it was empty. She then turned towards Mehul and saw him sitting with his eyes wide open, transfixed by a tarantula crawling casually along the wooden truss towards a large brown and black moth.

As the sounds of the rainforest began to penetrate her consciousness, she found herself tuning in to the vibrant chorus of the frogs and insects. The longer she focused on the sounds, the more sensitive her hearing became. She could hear the gentle patter of raindrops hitting the glass windows and ceiling, creating a soothing background noise that further immersed her in the beauty of the rainforest.

Suddenly, her ears picked up the sound of someone weeping across the room. She noticed a man with dark blonde hair, his head in his hands, weeping inconsolably. Mama Alandra sat beside him, trying to comfort him with her hands on his back.

Restlessness coursed through her veins, urging her to stand and stretch her legs. Walking around the temple room, a tingling sensation rippled through her calves, the energy of the space overwhelming her.

She stepped outside, the darkness obscuring the view of the forest, but she could still make out the outlines of trees, leaves, and branches illuminated by the soft glow of the candles that lined the temple. The soothing sounds of the crickets filled the air, overpowering the *icaros* that were being sung inside. She gazed at the trees, their gentle glow complemented by the fireflies floating around them. The rain fell in a soothing pattern against the leaves, the murmur of the crickets and the sound of the *icaros*. A sense of tranquillity enveloped her, like a warm, comforting blanket, and the distant rustling of leaves filled her with a profound sense of peace. The beauty of her surroundings tugged at the corners of her lips, and she smiled, feeling overwhelmed by gratitude for the experience. At that moment, she knew she was precisely where she was meant to be, surrounded by the natural majesty of the world.

Having completely lost track of time, she looked around, disoriented, searching for a clock. Just then, Juan approached her and caught her attention. Aaliyah gestured, indicating that she wanted to know the time, and Juan informed her that it was already 12:30 AM. She was taken aback by how swiftly time had passed while she was under the influence of the medicine. Juan asked if she was feeling alright, and she nodded slowly. He offered to accompany her back to her cottage, and they walked towards it in silence. She opened the door to her room to find Anshika asleep on the bed, snoring lightly. She crept in quietly, trying not to wake her friend, and settled down in her own bed to rest.

When she closed her eyes, a vivid image of a large, dark figure with piercing green eyes flashed in her mind, causing her to gasp. She sat up, realising it was only a hallucination and that the medicine was still affecting her. She braced herself for more intense visions and took a deep breath before sinking back into the soft, warm pillow and closing her eyes once again.

Reflections

The dining room was usually bustling with morning chatter, but today the clinking of cutlery filled the space. Everyone sat in silence, communicating only through their eyes. The mood was reflective and heavy, with an unspoken weight that hung in the air. No one felt like talking, or maybe everyone was failing to find the right words. Mama Aya's influence was still strong, and everyone felt her presence coursing through their veins.

Aaliyah struggled to focus on her plate of watermelon, her mind haunted by the previous night's events. She could hear the occasional sniffle and sigh from other tables, but she avoided eye contact to keep from getting dragged into any conversations. Suddenly, a voice broke the silence. "People are chattier at funerals," a woman from the next table remarked, and the room erupted in light laughter. It was a relief to have the tension broken, but the mood remained sombre.

After some time, Gauri spoke up, her voice hesitant as if she didn't want to interrupt the solemn atmosphere. "Where is Rehaan?"

"I tried waking him up, but he wanted to sleep more," Daniel replied, taking a bite of the banana.

"He left really early last evening, what happened to him?" Anshika asked, pushing her leftovers around on her plate.

"He had a really dark experience. He puked a lot and then kept crying. He wanted to talk to his parents. Mama Alandra and Juan tried to console him, but he wouldn't stop. Then Juan put him to bed in a room just outside the temple," Daniel explained.

The room fell silent again, the weight of the previous night's events hanging heavy in the air. Everyone ate in silence, lost in their own thoughts and memories.

Daniel turned to Anshika, who seemed deep in contemplation. "What about you, how was your experience?" he asked her. She sighed deeply and took a few moments before answering.

"I don't know. I'm still trying to figure it out. I didn't understand a lot of it. I've tried other psychedelics before, but this was much deeper. I might have seen the evolution of the human race and where we're headed. The future I saw was terrifying, to say the least. And I couldn't do anything but witness the destruction silently." Her voice cracked as she looked away, wiping away tears. Mehul patted her back lightly and squeezed her shoulder.

"Man, it was really intense for me too. I think I was talking to trees, and I might have interacted with some aliens. At some point, I realised I was the alien, and I was talking to myself in the mirror. Then every creature around me tried to attack me. I saw some gigantic spiders that chased me through the forest, and then I was saved by jumping into a waterfall. But I think the worst part for me was the puking. I must've puked five times. I felt like I was going to die in my last bout."

"Well, at least you didn't get diarrhoea like me," Anshika added sarcastically.

"I agree," sniggered Mehul. "I'd prefer puking any day over pooping in such a situation. What about you, Liya? You didn't poop or puke?"

"No, but I did bawl like a baby. It felt really good."

"You did? I didn't notice," said Mehul.

"Yeah, you were quite busy staring at the tarantula at that point."

"Fuck, that was real? I thought I was hallucinating."

Laughter filled the room, bringing back a sense of normalcy. As the guests finished their breakfast, Juan entered the kitchen and invited everyone to the integration session at the temple. Aaliyah and Mehul, done with their meals, proceeded to join the session.

"Are you okay, Liya?" Mehul asked as they walked out of the community kitchen.

"Hmm, I think so," she responded slowly, choking on her words.

"You don't always have to pretend to be strong, you know,"

Mehul said, his gaze fixed on her, while she deliberately averted her eyes. "You can open up and share what's on your mind."

Aaliyah kept her focus on the path ahead, her eyes swollen and red. "I'm at a loss for words," she confessed, her voice quivering. "But I can tell you that I've found some answers to my struggles."

Mehul placed a comforting hand on her shoulder. "I'm glad to hear that," he reassured her. "Remember, I'm here for you if you ever want to share anything." A weak smile graced Aaliyah's lips as she redirected her attention to the path ahead.

Upon entering the temple, the gentle embrace of warm sunlight and the enticing aroma of smoky tobacco enveloped them. Yet, amidst these pleasant sensations, a faint stench of vomit wafted through the air, originating from a corner near one of the windows. Mama Alandra, seated against the wall alongside Jorje and Juan, greeted the arriving participants with heartfelt smiles, gesturing for them to settle on the adjacent mattresses arranged in a shorter length.

After everyone had settled, Juan extended a warm welcome, his voice resonating through the room. "Good morning, friends! I hope that last evening's experience was meaningful for each of you." The space fell silent, prompting a chuckle from Juan. "This reaction is quite typical," he remarked, glancing around at the dazed expressions. "You were a lucky group because there was a strong presence of some powerful spirits that were protecting each one of you from the dark forces that were trying to disturb the session," he continued.

The mention of dark forces woke up the room, and whispers filled the space. "What kind of dark forces?" Mehul asked.

"The kind that can ruin the experience of the medicine and make life worse for the participant," Juan replied. "But we don't want to discuss the dark energies, because we were all protected by Mother Aya and the ancestors," he added quickly, forestalling any further questions about the dark energies. "Today's session is important. We want to understand how you can use the learnings from the medicine in your life," he said, his voice calm yet firm.

"We'll take turns going around the room, and I invite each of you to share your personal experiences," Juan announced, his voice carrying a sense of encouragement. "Reflect on what you've learned and how it has contributed to your growth." Upon concluding his introduction, he turned his attention to an extremely groggy Rehaan, who sat nearest to him, urging him to be the first to share his encounter with the group.

Nervously, he stumbled over his words. "I'm not sure exactly what happened last night. It started well, but then everything turned dark. I felt like I was dying. There were these beautiful creatures, but they ran away when I approached. After that, I started crying and felt like I couldn't breathe." He attempted to share details about his experience but failed to find the right words. Shortly after a few unsuccessful attempts, he started to weep and requested the person sitting next to him to continue until he could compose himself.

One by one, they shared their stories. The energy in the room oscillated between moments of excitement, with laughter and giggles filling the air, and somber moments, with individuals shedding tears as they recounted their dark experiences. When the last person finished, Mama Alandra addressed the group, with Juan translating her words. "I encourage each of you to write down your experiences and take time to reflect on them in the days ahead. Slowly integrate your learnings into your daily routines," she advised.

The group slowly began to disperse, with many of them thanking Mama Alandra and her family. The atmosphere in the room felt more tranquil following the integration session, and individuals began to exit the temple, lost in contemplation of their encounters with the medicine. While everyone was walking towards the door, Daniel walked over to Juan, who was picking up some bed sheets that were piled up against the wall near the door. Aaliyah and Mehul overheard their conversation, which was about the forest, and decide to join in.

"I'm just asking Juan about the forest and if he has any suggestions for any safe areas for our camp," Daniel translated when they finished conversing in rapid Portuguese.

"There is a place one hour from here that is safer than the rest. But I recommend you visit the forest during the day and return to the retreat at night. The forest is not safe for you," Juan hesitantly replied.

"Why not? What is the problem with camping in the forest?" asked Mehul, his curiosity piqued.

"The forest has become very protective of her land. She doesn't like outsiders anymore," Juan informed them casually. Aaliyah and Mehul exchanged a look and turned back to inquire further.

"What do you mean by that? Why does she not like outsiders?" asked Aaliyah calmly.

"People have become selfish and only take from the land. They leave trash, burn the forest, and cut down trees. Animals suffer and die. Everyone suffers. Local tribes can't find food, and animals can't find food. There is a lot of pain in the forest," Juan said, struggling to maintain his composure.

"We are watching the forest die a slow, painful death because outsiders come and take more than is needed. The forest is kind, but when more is taken and the balance is spoiled, then the forest fights back. Creatures protect the forest, and the outsiders are hurt," Juan continued, his voice filled with passion.

"Did anyone die in the forest?" Mehul asked impatiently.

"Not recently, but many outsiders who tried to stay in the forest at night would run away with fear," Juan shared in a hushed tone.

"And the forest is okay with the tribe's people?" asked Daniel in a slightly condescending tone.

"Yes, because they don't harm the forest," Juan responded, smiling slightly.

Daniel became visibly irritated with Juan's response, adding, "I have camped in the forest many times. I went there two years ago and stayed for four days. Nothing happened."

"The forest changes every day because outsiders are hurting it more and more. Much has changed from two years ago," Juan replied firmly.

"What happens to the outsiders who stay in the forest? What scares them?" asked Aaliyah to break the tension between them. Juan sensed that his warnings were not going to change their plans, so he started walking out of the room with the pile of bedsheets in his hand and ended the conversation with his final comment.

"They experience their worst fears."

Daniel let out a sarcastic laugh when Juan left the temple and turned towards Aaliyah and Mehul, who looked concerned. "Dramatic, huh! Don't worry guys, the locals have a habit of exaggerating and scaring tourists. We'll be fine."

The three friends walked back to their cottage, deep in thought about their upcoming camping trip in the forest.

While walking over the lotus pond, their attention was drawn to the sound of the macaws' wings flapping, echoing through the air. Aaliyah turned to look and saw the brightly coloured birds perched on a tree. She felt a sense of awe at their beauty, but it was short-lived as she noticed people gathering around the tree with cameras and phones. "Ugh, why do people have to be so intrusive?" she muttered under her breath.

The trio stopped to watch the beautiful birds, but their attention was quickly diverted by a loud crack. They walked closer to the tree to find a man attempting to climb a low branch of a neighbouring tree, causing it to snap. The sound frightened the macaws, and they flew away into the forest. The crowd dispersed, disappointed at not being able to get closer to the birds.

Mehul smirked and said, "I don't think they've experienced Mother Aya yet." Aaliyah looked at him quizzically, and he continued, "The forest has a way of showing people the consequences of their actions. It's like a mother protecting her child.

"How have we become so insensitive?" Aaliyah asked rhetorically, feeling disheartened by the behaviour of the crowd. While walking back to their cottage, her unease about their camping trip in the forest lingered. She turned to Daniel and asked, "Are you certain about camping in the forest?"

"Of course, Liya. Don't worry, we'll be careful," Daniel replied, trying to reassure her with a grin.

Mehul added, "Plus, we'll respect the forest and its inhabitants. We'll leave no trace."

Her mind was still clouded with doubts, but she didn't want to dampen the spirits of her friends by expressing her apprehension. Upon entering their cottage, the group immediately started packing their camping gear, scattering a range of equipment throughout the room.

It was a mishmash of well-worn and well-loved items that had seen them through many adventures. The sturdy canvas tents were weather-beaten but reliable, with durable zippers that could withstand even the harshest of elements. The sleeping bags were plush and warm, offering a cosy respite from the chill of the night air. The group worked in harmony, each member knowing their role and contributing to the efficient packing of their gear. Aaliyah's apprehension slowly gave way to a growing sense of anticipation, and she couldn't help but smile as she realised that this trip would be another unforgettable adventure with her closest friends.

When they finished packing up their gear, Aaliyah gazed out of the window, her eyes fixed on the dense forest that loomed in the distance. A mix of excitement and trepidation coursed through her veins, a feeling that she couldn't quite shake off. The forest seemed to stretch on forever, its dark and mysterious depths hinting at untold secrets and hidden dangers. Even though Aaliyah tried to push the warning that Juan had given them to the back of her mind, she couldn't help but feel a knot of unease tighten in her stomach. A part of her was eager to explore the wilderness, to lose herself in the natural beauty of the world and forget about the worries and stresses of everyday life. But another part of her was all too aware of the risks involved, the many ways that things could go wrong, leaving them stranded and alone in the unforgiving wilderness.

Core

The car drove through the winding roads that snaked through the dense forest. The air was heavy with the sweet aroma of blooming flowers and the constant buzz of insects. The lush green canopy of the forest stretched out as far as the eye could see, and Gauri couldn't contain her excitement.

"This is so exciting!" she exclaimed, leaning forward to catch a better view of the forest. "How far are we from the campsite?" she inquired.

"Ha ha, there is no designated campsite. We have to make one," Daniel explained as he deftly steered the car around some construction debris.

"Could you play some music?" Rehaan asked over his shoulder, trying to capture the beauty of the forest on his camera.

"Enjoy the sounds of the jungle, man!" Anshika snapped back in an irritable tone.

"OK, OK, relax," Rehaan said, turning back to his camera.

Daniel slowed the car down after about an hour, and they began looking for a path into the forest.

"Can't you use maps to find a way in?" Gauri asked

"Ha ha, not yet. But I'm sure that'll happen in a few years," Daniel laughed, looking around.

While driving along the winding dirt road, Daniel spotted a family of tribals walking towards them. He slowed down the jeep and called out to them, asking for directions. As the family approached, they quickened their pace to avoid any conversation with the outsiders. Daniel stopped the car and called out to the man again. The family looked at the group with suspicion, eyeing them warily. Daniel persisted and requested the man to come closer to the jeep. After some persuasion, the man reluctantly walked towards them and asked where they were headed.

Daniel informed him of their plan to camp in the forest, causing the man's expression to change from suspicion to fear. While Daniel conversed with the man, trying to convince him, Aaliyah kept her gaze fixed on the woman standing behind him. The woman cradled her toddler in a cloth that covered her bare chest. The little one clung tightly to her mother's colourful beaded necklace, attempting to hide in her thick mane.

After several minutes of rapid interaction, the family walked away from the jeep. "These tribals are hard to crack," said Daniel exasperated.

"Did he tell you the way?" asked Mehul.

"Sort of, but I can't bank on it," replied Daniel.

"Why not?" inquired Anshika.

"He kept saying that we shouldn't camp in the forest. Finally, when I told him that we will leave before nightfall, he told me a place we could camp for a while."

"Daniel, are you sure it's safe to camp in the forest?" asked Anshika, concerned.

"Of course, I know what I'm doing," he said as he raced the jeep through the winding roads.

They continued down the road for several minutes, with their heads sticking out of the windows, desperately searching for a way into the forest. The sounds of the jungle overpowered the silence that pervaded the jeep. The rustling of leaves and chirping of birds created a natural symphony, but the group couldn't shake off the anxiety that had taken hold.

"There it is!" shouted Daniel with excitement.

Turning onto a forest track, they drove slowly through the forest, trying to find the perfect spot to set up camp. The revving of the engine echoed through the forest, overpowering the sounds of the jungle. After some time, they arrived at a clearing big enough for their camp. Daniel stopped the car at the edge of the clearing, and they all hopped out and began unloading the camping equipment.

They set up four tents, with the front facing the magnificent forest and the back facing the jeep. After setting up their tents, Mehul and Aaliyah decided to explore the forest. They walked deeper into the woods while the chattering monkeys swung effortlessly through the trees, guiding their path. The forest was quiet, and the only sounds were the rustling of leaves under their feet and the occasional call of a bird.

While walking, the distant roar of a waterfall caught their attention. They followed the sound and arrived at a small stream that flowed into a pool at the base of a rocky outcrop.

"Wow, this is incredible!" Mehul exclaimed, staring at the sparkling water.

"It's like a hidden gem," Aaliyah replied, smiling.

They sat by the stream, enjoying the soothing sounds of water and rustling leaves. After spending some time by the stream, they decide to return to their campsite. Aaliyah marvelled at the beauty of their surroundings as they walked cautiously over the soft bed of the forest floor and couldn't resist saying, "This place is unbelievable."

Mehul couldn't help but boast, "I think some thanks are in order."

She replied sheepishly, "Yes, you can thank me for planning the trip."

He chuckled, "Yeah, thank you for not pooping on the plan."

While walking around a massive ant hill, the two laughed.

Mehul stopped to capture some photographs of passion flowers while Aaliyah bent down to tie her laces. Suddenly, there was a rattling sound from behind a tree close to Mehul. Aaliyah crouched on the forest floor, listening intently for the source of the sound.

"What was that?" she asked.

"What was what?"

"That sound, didn't you hear it?" she asked again. The rattling repeated, and this time it sounded closer.

"Did you hear it? I think it came from that side," she said, pointing towards him.

He replied, "Yeah, I heard that. What could it be?"

She asked, "You want to look for what it is?"

"Are you crazy? Let's walk back. Remember, we are the intruders here."

The rattling repeated, and Aaliyah looked towards Mehul. She noticed him fiddling with something in his pockets. "You're such an idiot! Why would you do that?"

He chuckled as he revealed a vibrant pink plastic toy. "Sorry, Liya, you know how much I enjoy teasing you."

She rolled her eyes and turned around to walk back. "Let's go back now."

They walked back to the campsite and found Daniel and Anshika making a small fire a little away from the tents. The group spent the rest of the day sitting around the fire, taking photographs, playing games, and preparing dinner for the evening.

* * *

The stillness of the night was interrupted by an odd sound, causing Aaliyah to awaken abruptly from her light slumber. She lay still in her sleeping bag, listening intently. After a few moments, she heard a rustling of leaves nearby and the same rattling sound.

Anshika, sensing Aaliyah's unease, whispered, "Did you hear that?"

"I did," Aaliyah whispered back.

"Do you want to peek outside to see what it was?" Anshika asked.

"You know that's how characters start dying in horror movies, right?" Aaliyah replied, half-jokingly.

"Shut up, Liya. Look, someone put on the flashlight," Anshika whispered, hearing the unzipping of a tent. They cautiously unzipped their own tent and peered outside.

Aaliyah's stern look cut through the silence, "Did you make that sound, Mehul?" she demanded.

Mehul's voice quavered with fear as he replied, "Are you crazy? No!" Beads of sweat dripped down his forehead, and the torch in his trembling hand flickered like a dying flame.

"What was that?" stuttered Rehaan, poking his head out of his tiny tent.

"I have no idea. It could be a snake or foxes," responded Daniel flashing his torch through the forest.

Daniel and Mehul stepped out of the tent to investigate. They walked around for some time, flashing the torch all around the campsite. After failing to uncover any signs of danger, Daniel proceeded to relight the bonfire as a means of deterring any potential intruders.

"Whatever it was, it's gone. The fire should keep them away," Daniel said, reassuringly.

"Sweet dreams, everyone," Mehul said as he stepped back into his tent.

With the sun's ascent, the forest came to life with the sweet chirping of birds and the gentle filtering of the morning sun rays through the towering rubber trees. The group savoured a peaceful morning by sipping coffee and munching on energy bars and slices of bread with jam. While the group chattered away, Daniel's voice boomed through their conversations, "There's a small lake nearby that we could visit. It's a birdwatcher's paradise." Without hesitation, he hoisted his camera bag over his shoulder and added, "We can walk there."

The group set off on their walk, the rustling of leaves and the crunching of twigs beneath their feet breaking the serenity of the forest. The path was lined with towering rubber trees that swayed with the gentle breeze, creating a soothing rhythm that accompanied their footsteps. Walking deeper into the forest, they were awestruck at the beauty that surrounded them as the chatter slowly dissipated.

Finally, after a 20-minute walk, the group emerged into a small clearing where a breathtaking lake lay before them. The thicket of rubber trees surrounding the lake created a natural barrier that amplified the stillness of the area. Small mammals darted towards the trees on the other side as they approached the water's edge, fleeing from the commotion of their arrival. The sounds of nature soon gave way to the clicks of cameras and the laughter of the group.

Splitting into two groups, they set off to explore the perimeter of the lake, scanning the treetops for any signs of the feathered residents that called this place home. Their eyes darted back and forth, scanning every inch of the forest in search of movement. While walking around the lake, their excitement grew with each new discovery. They spotted birds of every hue, snakes slithering along the branches, and even a sloth bear lazily making its way through the trees. With each sighting, they paused to capture the moment, their cameras clicking in unison. Finally, exhausted from their exploration, the group found a cosy spot to relax and bask in the tranquillity of the surroundings.

"I'm going to swim in the lake," declared Rehaan, taking off his shirt.

Daniel placed his hand on Rehaan's shoulder and cautioned him, "Slow down buddy, it's not a good idea. There are creatures that live underwater that you may not want to encounter."

Rehaan shrugged off Daniel's warning, "Come on, it can't be that bad."

Daniel replied, "Well, there is a parasitic fish called Candiru that swims up the urethra and feeds on it. It's only found in these waters."

Rehaan's eyes bulged out of their sockets as he listened in horror to the graphic description. In a frantic attempt to compose himself, he quickly tucked in his shirt and plopped back down on the sheet that was spread out on the forest floor. After the group dissolved into giggles, Rehaan felt like a fish out of water. Eventually, the laughter subsided, and the group settled by the serene lake. Rehaan snapped pictures of the forest and the group's comically futile attempts of starting a fire with twigs and leaves. After a while, he grew bored and felt the urge to explore. Grabbing his camera and tripod, he hiked to the opposite side of the lake, hoping to capture some stunning shots. Suddenly, the gang's lively chatter was interrupted by a piercing scream.

"OWW!"

"OWWWW! What the hell is that?" Rehaan yelled from the other side of the lake.

"What happened? Is that for the camera?" Mehul chuckled.

"What the hell?" Dropping his camera, Rehaan dashed back to where everyone was sitting, attempting to brush something off his back.

"My back is burning!" He shrieked, pulling up his shirt, and turned his back towards the group. Everyone stared at his back, horrified.

"What is it?" Rehaan screamed.

Daniel composed himself and tried to take charge of the situation. "Okay, you need to calm down. It's not good, but we'll remove them."

"Them? What are they?" Rehaan squealed again.

"Parasitic bugs," Aaliyah whispered.

Daniel pulled out a pair of gloves from his fanny pack and started removing the blood-sucking bugs from his back. After removing all the bugs, he sprayed some antiseptic oil on his back and gave him some water to drink.

"It's time to go back," whispered Daniel. Everyone agreed and began walking back towards the camp in silence.

"Are those bugs common?" Anshika asked Daniel, breaking the uncomfortable silence.

"No, I've never seen or heard of them before, but given the number of undiscovered species in this forest, it's not surprising," he responded.

Upon arriving at their campsite, they find fruits and berries scattered around the car, and their tents smeared with dirt. "Shit, now what happened here?" Mehul exclaimed irritably.

In a composed tone, Daniel informed the group, "Monkeys"

While the group was engrossed in clearing the area, a sudden shrill cry pierced through the air, startling everyone. Gauri's sudden outburst of disgust made the group halt and turn towards her direction.

Their wide-eyed gazes were fixated on an unsettling sight - the lifeless body of a massive rodent, its skin mottled with shades of dark orange and yellow, and swarming with an infestation of repulsive worms. Approaching the carcass, they felt a wave of nausea hit them when they took in the grotesque sight. After inspecting the remains carefully, Daniel took hold of a sizeable stick and used it to prod the carcass out of the campsite, making sure to keep a safe distance from the filthy scavengers.

"Let's leave tomorrow morning. Something is off about this place," he suggested in a concerned tone. The group agreed, and they decided to call it an early night and leave the next morning.

* * *

Aaliyah stirred in her sleeping bag, her eyes blinking open to a faint fluttering sound outside her tent. She lay still, her ears perked up, trying to locate the source of the sound. Then, she heard it again, the sound of something moving outside her tent. She cautiously peered through the small opening and gasped when she saw a massive butterfly glowing in the colours of the sunrise—purple and yellow—perched on the Jeep nearby. It was a sight that took her breath away, and she knew she had to capture it in a photograph. Slowly, she unzipped her tent, trying not to startle the butterfly. She stepped out and tiptoed towards the butterfly, hoping to get closer for a better shot. The butterfly took flight, and she hurriedly chased after it, walking deeper into the forest.

She could feel her heart beating faster with excitement as she crouched to take the photo. She steadied her hands, poised to capture the colourful butterfly perched on the nearby flower. Suddenly, a rustling sound broke the serene silence behind her. She turned around, expecting to see a curious animal, but there was nothing there. Looking back at the butterfly, her heart sank at the sight of its absence.

Missing the opportunity left her disappointed but as she walked through the dense foliage, the lush beauty of the forest began to captivate her once again. The towering trees seemed to stretch endlessly into the sky, their branches interlocking to form a natural canopy that filtered the sunlight. The soft rustling of leaves, the chirping of birds, and the distant gurgling of a nearby stream filled the air, creating a tranquil symphony of nature. She felt a sense of awe and wonder at the majesty of the Amazon. She marvelled at the intricate patterns on the petals of the flowers that bloomed in every direction. The vibrant colours and fragrant scents enveloped her senses, transporting her to a world of pure beauty and serenity. Despite the unexpected end to their camping trip, she felt a sense of gratitude for the two days of immersion in this magnificent paradise.

As she ventured further, her anxiety intensified, fueled by the absence of human sounds in the vicinity of the camp. Fear pulsed through her as she questioned whether she had strayed too far from the group. The forest was coming alive with the sounds of birds, but the feeling of isolation and disorientation persisted. With each step, her heart pounded in her chest, and a sinking feeling weighed her down. The lush, green canopy of the jungle, once a symbol of vibrant beauty, now closed in around her, suffocating and oppressive. Her hopes of reuniting with her group dwindled with every passing moment, leaving her in a state of growing despair.

Her mind was in turmoil, thoughts whirling like a violent storm as the struggle to recall the way back to the camp intensified. She couldn't help but berate herself for not paying closer attention to the landmarks around her. The forest floor was uneven and treacherous, making every step a challenge as she pushed forward. Every twist and turn of the winding forest path seemed to blur together, leaving her disoriented and lost.

Despite her best efforts, she couldn't shake the feeling that she was hopelessly lost. Every step she took seemed to lead her deeper into the unknown, further from safety and the comforting familiarity of the camp. Stumbling forward, her feet beginning to ache from the constant walking, hot tears welled up in her eyes. The frustration and fear that had been simmering beneath the surface now threatened to boil over, and she felt a hot tear trickle down her cheek. The thought of being lost in the vast and unknown jungle was too much to bear, and she couldn't help but wonder if she would ever make it back to safety.

She had walked for what felt like hours, and yet, she was nowhere near her destination. The lush foliage seemed to stretch endlessly in every direction, and she couldn't help but wonder how much further she had to go. Her panic escalated with each passing moment, and her mind raced with worst-case scenarios. Despite the fear that threatened to consume her, she pressed on, determined to find her way back to her friends. The forest was alive with the gentle sounds of nature, but it offered no solace to her troubled mind. She continued to walk, hoping against hope that she would soon find her companions and return to the safety of the campsite. She searched for anything familiar that could lead her back, but everything looked the same—the towering trees, the thick bush, and the unforgiving terrain.

In the moment of despair, she sought solace in her trusty phone, hoping it could provide a glimmer of relief. But alas, her hopes were quickly dashed when she realised there was no signal to be found. With no means of reaching her friends, she was left to face her predicament alone, feeling more stranded than a castaway on a deserted island.

The fear inside her continued to grow until she couldn't control it any more. She screamed for help, calling out the names of her friends, but all she heard were her own echoes. She tried this several times, yelling out each of their names, but no one answered her desperate calls.

She was alone, with nothing but her useless phone and the vast, intimidating forest.

Encounter

Trembling with fear, she sat on the unforgiving forest floor, enveloped by an overwhelming silence that only amplified the pounding of her heart. Her throat was parched, and her muscles ached from hours of aimless wandering through the dense, towering trees. Glancing at her watch with trembling hands, she felt a sickening knot form in her stomach as she realized it was already 9 a.m.. Panic surged through her as the realisation dawned that she had been lost for four hours, but it felt like an eternity.

Every direction seemed like an endless, twisting maze with no visible escape. Her mind raced with all the possible consequences of being stranded alone in the unforgiving jungle, and she couldn't shake off the feeling of impending doom.

Looking around at the endless forest, she felt a sense of hopelessness wash over her. She wondered how she would survive in this vast and unfamiliar wilderness. Her mind was numb, her thoughts jumbled, and her heart was pounding in her chest. She hoped that her friends would find her if she stayed in one place, but the uncertainty of her situation made her feel even more anxious. She screamed for help every few minutes, hoping for a response, but all she heard was the sound of her own voice echoing through the trees. She felt her energy draining away while she walked around aimlessly, trying to find her way back to the campsite. But the more she walked, the more lost she felt. The forest seemed to be closing in on her, suffocating her with its silence and shadows.

She turned to her phone, desperate for some kind of guidance, but all she could find were names and images of edible fruits and berries that she could find in the forest. She remembered that she had some food and water in her cargo pants. She searched her pockets and found two energy bars, a small bottle of water, and some tissues. Nibbling on the protein bar she felt her energy levels slowly rising, but her fear remained.

Despite her exhaustion, she refused to give up. She knew that she had to keep moving and keep searching for a way out. For thirty long minutes, she trudged on through the unrelenting jungle, her steps slow and heavy with every passing moment. She walked with no clear direction in mind, her only hope to stumble upon some sign of civilization or a faint signal on her phone. Every few minutes, she would glance down at her device with desperate eyes, hoping to find a glimmer of hope. But the thick canopy of trees overhead seemed to block any chance of a signal. The dense forest seemed to mock her as if it was determined to keep her lost and alone in its unforgiving embrace. The weight of her situation was crushing her, and she collapsed on the ground, feeling completely helpless and hopeless.

She cursed under her breath, the frustration and fear building within her. "Stupid butterfly is going to be the death of me," she muttered through gritted teeth, her voice shaking with fear. She cried out to Mother Aya, hoping for some divine intervention, some way out of this nightmare.

"I don't deserve to die like this," her body shook with fear as she whispered to herself.

Her inner critic chimed in, the voice cruel and biting. "You deserve this," it taunted.

Her mind raced, and she cried out in frustration, "Why do I always end up in these situations?"

The inner critic replied with a sneer, "Because you love it."

Tears streamed down her face as she tried to explain, "I didn't choose this."

"Of course you did, you always choose wrong," the critic retorted.

With frustration boiling within her, she let out a scream, "Just shut up! I don't have time for this!" Her body trembled.

Looking up at the towering trees, she suddenly felt a shift. A surreal calm enveloped her as she saw the beauty of the forest. She laughed through her tears, recognizing the absurdity of her situation, "This is the most Amazonian experience I could have asked for." She leaned against a tree, watching the forest's creatures go about their lives, oblivious to her struggles. She felt the weight of her past traumas as memories of her childhood came flooding back to her.

She was just eight years old when her parents were faced with a difficult decision. They had to travel extensively for work, and they could not take her with them. Against Aaliyah's wishes, they made the tough choice to send her away to live with her strict aunt and grumpy uncle. Her aunt's home was a far cry from the warmth and comfort of her own. Instead, it was a place of oppression and fear, where she felt like a prisoner.

She felt utterly alone and vulnerable, and her cousin made her life a living hell. At first, he seemed sweet and caring, someone she could look up to, but slowly, his true nature was revealed. He would watch movies with her when his parents weren't around, and then touch her in ways that made her feel uncomfortable and violated.

Her world had become a waking nightmare, and she was trapped within its clutches for an agonising month. She was unable to tell anyone about the horrors that she was enduring, her voice silenced by fear and shame. Her parents, oblivious to her suffering, callously urged her to extend her stay and remain in the care of her aunt.

But Aaliyah knew that she couldn't endure it any longer. She was suffocating in a web of abuse and torment that seemed to grow tighter with each passing day. And so, with trembling hands and a heavy heart, she gathered her courage and ran away from her aunt's house. For two long days, she was untraceable, lost in a world of fear and uncertainty. Her parents desperately searched for her, fearing the worst. When she finally contacted them, it was with a voice that trembled with terror and despair. She would only return home if they promised to take her away from that accursed place. Her parents heaved a sigh of relief, but their relief was short-lived. Her father was furious at her behaviour and grounded her for two long months. But for Aaliyah, it was a small price to pay for her freedom.

Her mother, desperate to understand what had driven her daughter to such extreme measures, tried to probe her for answers. But she could never bring herself to speak of the horrors she had endured, the shame and fear still choking her voice.

As Aaliyah sat amidst the lush and vibrant Amazonian jungle, tears streamed down her face, carrying with them the weight of her past traumas. The sounds of nature surrounded her, the rustling of leaves and the chirping of birds, providing a stark contrast to the darkness within her. As she relived the horrors of her past, a feeling of despair overtook her. But then, something shifted within her. She wiped away her tears and reminded herself that she was her own protector, that she had the strength to find a way out of this perilous situation. "Crying is pointless, Aaliyah. Don't be weak," she admonished herself. With a parched throat and limited water, she couldn't afford to lose any more strength.

Brushing off the dirt from her pants, she got up and began walking again, trying to determine the correct path to take. "Think, Aaliyah, THINK!" she scolded herself, her voice cracking with frustration. "How could you be so stupid? Why didn't you mark your path? Why did you follow that butterfly? Are you 5? You can't do anything properly! You call yourself a good planner—look what you got yourself into! Now plan your way out of this mess!"

She could feel her confidence slipping away with every passing moment. She could feel her heart sinking as she realised that she might be lost in the jungle forever. But she knew she couldn't give up. There was a battle happening inside her, a battle between fear and determination. Calling out for help, she walked briskly through the woods, her ears straining to hear any kind of human sounds. Walking through the woods, she listened intently, trying to identify any sign of civilization. Suddenly, she heard the leaves rustling behind her. Her heart pounded in her chest, and she turned around quickly. But there was nothing there.

Continuing on her path, she walked faster, feeling a presence behind her. Glancing over her shoulder every few steps, she quickened her pace, feeling a growing sense of unease. Suddenly, a sharp crack echoed just a few metres away, causing her heart to skip a beat. With a mounting sense of dread, she whirled around to investigate the source of the noise, only to be confronted by the unrelenting expanse of the forest, looming ominously in front of her. Chills ran down her spine, and her heart raced as she sensed the unmistakable feeling of being followed. Picking up the pace, the presence behind her grew stronger, urging her to run. With every beat of her heart, she could feel the heat rising in her body as she pushed herself to the limit. But the pursuit was relentless, and she knew that she couldn't keep this up for long. Fear gnawed at her, making her hesitant to look back. The humidity of the forest air clung to her skin, making each step feel heavier than the last.

Despite the overwhelming urge to collapse, she kept moving forward, knowing that her survival depended on it. Her mind was at war with itself, torn between the instinct to flee and the hopelessness of her situation. Her legs started to give out beneath her, but giving up was inconceivable. She had to keep going, even if it meant facing certain death. Suddenly, the vines snared her feet, and she tumbled to the ground, face down on the damp forest floor. She braced herself for the predator to strike, and for a moment, time stood still. Her heart raced as she braced for impact, but nothing happened.

Minutes passed, and still, no attack. Slowly and hesitantly, she turned to her side, hoping to regain her footing and escape this nightmare. As she opened her eyes, she saw it towering over her, a monstrous dark figure with piercing green eyes and razor-sharp teeth. The sight was too much to bear, and she recoiled, falling back onto the forest floor. As darkness crept into her vision, she knew that this was it. The end.

Shadow

Plummeting through an endless abyss of blinding white light, her heart raced with fear and uncertainty. She felt weightless and untethered, as though she were floating in a void of nothingness. Her consciousness returned abruptly as her body hit the damp, soft ground. A million thoughts ran through her foggy mind.

Am I dead? Is this the afterlife? What will happen to Hex? How will Mum and Dad handle this? How will bhai handle this? Why did I follow that butterfly? Why am I still thinking about my human life if I am dead? Oh god, my arm hurts. Have I been sleeping? I need water. If I am alive, then I will definitely die of hunger or dehydration soon.

Gradually, Aaliyah's senses began to return, and she heard the gentle rustling of leaves and distant birdsong.

"Where am I?" she wondered, her mind consumed with a jumble of thoughts and emotions. She opened her eyes gradually and took in the sight of the dense, humid forest around her. The air felt thick and oppressive. Aaliyah's parched throat burned with every breath, and her vision was blurry and unfocused.

"What happened to me?" she muttered to herself, trying to piece together her memories. "Why does my head hurt so much?" she moaned, wincing at the dull ache in her skull.

Lying there on the ground, she suddenly remembered the dark creature with piercing green eyes and razor-sharp teeth. "Did I really see it?" she whispered to herself, unsure if it was real or just her imagination. Her heart pounded in her chest as she tried to piece together what had happened. Why hadn't the monster killed her? Had it simply left her for dead, or was there some other reason? A million thoughts and questions swirled around her mind, each one more confusing and terrifying than the last. Despite the pain in her arm and the urgent need for water, she found herself unable to move. She lay there, paralysed with fear and uncertainty, wondering what her fate would be. Would she ever see her family again? Would she be able to survive in this harsh and unforgiving wilderness?

Finally, summoning all her strength, she slowly sat up, feeling every nerve in her body come to life with a sharp, tingling sensation. The canopy of trees overhead seemed to loom ominously, casting dark shadows on the forest floor. She knew that she had to find water and try to make her way out of the forest, but the task seemed impossible.

Her eyes welled up with tears at the thought of her family and her beloved pet, Hex. Would they ever know what had become of her? Would they ever find her? She took a deep breath and tried to steady herself, staring blankly at the endless forest as she wondered if she had really seen the dark creature. Just as she was preparing to stand, she turned to her side and there it was—the ominous dark beast, with piercing green eyes fixed upon her. She gazed at the beast in wonder, struggling to identify it.

Was it a panther? No, it was too large for that. It was even bigger than a lion. It was, in fact, the biggest black cat she had ever seen. She gazed at the animal, uncertain of what to do next. Meanwhile, the beast looked down at its paws, where a large leaf was neatly laid out on the forest floor. The leaf was laden with passion fruits, berries, and nuts—a feast waiting just for her.

Aaliyah was confused. Was this real? Had the animal brought her food? Or was this a ploy to feed her before it attacked? Her mind raced with questions, but as the animal looked up at her, something changed. There was a softness in its eyes that she had not seen before. Despite its massive size and imposing presence, she couldn't help but find something endearing about the cat, particularly its enormous paws.

Her stomach growled and churned with hunger as she stared at the leaf decorated with passion fruits, berries, and nuts. Her eyes widened with disbelief and suspicion, for it seemed too good to be true. With trembling hands and an uneasy heart, she crawled towards the leaf, wary of the lurking predator that had brought her this feast.

With trembling hands, she picked up the passion fruit, her gaze locked onto the creature's piercing green eyes. A wave of fear washed over her, but the citrusy, sweet aroma of the fruit drew her in. The vibrant, bright yellow and orange pulp inside tantalised her taste buds, and she couldn't resist taking a bite. Suddenly, her body was consumed with pleasure. The explosion of flavours and fragrances was like a rainbow of sensations, vibrant and electric, a symphony for the senses. Each bite was like an awakening, a liberation, and she felt every nerve in her body come alive. The flavours and textures were so unfamiliar yet so alluring that she couldn't get enough.

For a moment, she forgot her perilous situation and lost herself in the feast. The colours were intense and vivid, the passion fruit's yellow pulp was bursting with brightness against the dark green of the jungle. The berries were like sparkling gems, ruby red and glistening in the sunlight filtering through the leaves. She felt like a ravenous beast, devouring each morsel with reckless abandon until nothing was left.

She had never tasted anything so divine or otherworldly. It was as if the jungle itself had provided her with this gift, a moment of respite and sustenance in the midst of her struggles. And if this were to be her last meal, then she would embrace death with open arms, grateful for the brief taste of paradise in this vast and unforgiving forest.

As the flavours of the delicious meal dissipated in her mouth, her anxiety returned with a vengeance, leaving her wondering what would happen next. She sat there, her heart pounding in her chest, waiting for the monster to make a move. The beast remained still, its piercing green eyes fixed on her as if studying her every move. She couldn't tell if it was amused or angry, but she couldn't shake the feeling that she was being watched.

She tried to muster the courage to move, to run, but her body refused to cooperate. Fear had taken hold of her, rendering her powerless. Her mind raced with thoughts of escape and survival while she sat there staring at the monster. She wondered if she could outrun the massive beast or climb a tree to safety. But every scenario she played out in her head ended with the beast catching her. She felt trapped, like a cornered animal. The panther's unblinking gaze continued to bear down on her, and her mind began to play tricks on her.

She imagined the beast chuckling to itself, amused by her futile plans of escape. Her heart raced trying to think of a way out, but her mind was clouded with fear.

Minutes felt like hours as the panther remained motionless, its eyes never leaving her. She felt like a prisoner, trapped in a nightmare from which she couldn't wake up. In a flash, the panther got up and moved gracefully towards the trees. She let out a sigh of relief, but the feeling was short-lived. Her heart sank as she gazed at the towering beast with its thick, gleaming black coat, almost as big as a horse. How could she ever escape it? When the panther glanced back at her, a soft roar escaped its throat, sending shivers down her spine. She muttered bitterly to herself, "I'm a prisoner now. Wonderful."
    With trembling legs, she struggled to her feet and stumbled towards the panther. She did her best to avoid touching any part of its long, thick black tail, which slithered across the forest floor like a black mamba. The panther continued to lead her deeper into the woods.

Walking through a denser part of the forest, she couldn't help but notice the eerie calm. The monkeys on the branches seemed unperturbed, peacefully munching on berries and staring at her. She couldn't help but wonder, "What the hell is happening in this jungle? Why isn't anyone going crazy with this scary predator strolling through the forest?"

Lost in thought, she didn't even consider where the monster was taking her. She simply followed it, still trying to make sense of the strange calmness of the forest. After several minutes of walking, the sound of a stream in the distance broke her trance.

Peering ahead while dodging the panther's massive head, she saw a freshwater stream running across the jungle.

As they approached the stream, her eyes widened in awe at the sight before her. The sparkling, crystal-clear water flowed over a rocky outcrop that formed a miniature waterfall. She fell to her knees, instinctively splashing the cool water on her face and taking several long sips. The water tasted like the purest mountain spring she had ever drunk from, just like the ones she remembered from her childhood in the Himalayas.

"Thank you," she whispered to the animal, who stared back at her blankly. Gracefully, it bent down towards the stream and drank, its green eyes never leaving her face. She knelt there, transfixed by the panther's otherworldly beauty. After some time, they resumed their journey, and she wondered where they were headed. "How long is this going to go on?" she thought to herself. They walked deeper into the woods, and she marvelled at the sights around her. The trees towered above, their branches rustling in the breeze, and the forest floor was covered in a carpet of vibrant wildflowers.

Finally, they arrived at a clearing, and Aaliyah gasped at the overwhelming view before her. A calm lake lay at the foot of a short range of hills, its surface shimmering like a million diamonds in the sun. The panther sat near the lake and turned its head to look at her, silently urging her to follow. She complied, sitting near the edge of the water and staring out at the serene vista. The panic she had felt earlier was replaced with a sense of wonder and peace.

While marvelling at the natural beauty around her, she noticed a family of otters frolicking in the water, a group of monkeys darting along the shore and tossing berries at each other, and colourful flocks of macaws soaring overhead, their feathers glinting in the sunlight. The scene seemed to have come straight out of a fairytale, and she was awestruck by the immersive experience of the jungle.

"I wish I had my phone to take a photograph. My phone!" She quickly fished out her phone from her pocket and noticed the time.

4 PM

"SHIT! The sun is going to set soon, how will I survive the night?" she wondered. Her hands shook while she stared at the phone, the one source of hope she had left, only to see that it was practically useless. She clutched it tightly, feeling a lump form in her throat. "What am I going to do?" she whispered to herself. The panic grew stronger with each passing moment, her body fidgeting as her mind raced with thoughts of being lost and alone in the vast wilderness with a monstrous beast.

"Where will I sleep? How will I stay safe? How will I ever find my way out of here?" Tears streamed down her face, her attempts to wipe them away in vain. Suddenly, a presence loomed beside her. She turned to see the towering figure of the panther. It was time to go. She took a deep breath, attempting to calm herself as she followed the beast's lead. They began walking back towards the trees, with the panther taking turns every couple of minutes.

Pushing deeper into the dense forest, she struggled to keep

up with the beast. Her mind was still consumed with fear and uncertainty, she followed the panther with a heavy heart, weakly putting one foot in front of the other, her thoughts spiralling out of control. Would anyone come looking for her? And if they did, would they believe her story? Her mind drifted to the comforts of her old life, the noise of traffic, the polluted air, and the familiar sounds of the city. She longed for them. After half a day of being lost in the jungle, she realised she had been fooling herself about being a country girl. She was nothing but a spoiled city brat, hopelessly addicted to the toxic lifestyle she had left behind.

Lost in her thoughts she barely noticed the familiar clearing they entered. Her pensive pondering came to an abrupt end when she spotted a backpack abandoned on the forest floor. Looking up, she saw several empty bottles scattered around, a bedsheet carelessly thrown on the ground, and the remnants of a recently extinguished bonfire. Her heart was filled with hope, thinking that she must be close to finding her humans. However, as she searched the area, a sinking feeling overcame her, realizing they were nowhere to be found. Reality hit her, and her heart sank.

They were gone.

Desert

The weight of betrayal pressed down on her shoulders, and she fell to her knees, unable to hold back the flood of emotions any longer.

"Why would they leave me?" she cried out, her words choked with emotion, as the pain of abandonment tore at her soul. The forest resounded with her anguished howls, each one a release of pent-up agony that had been building within for years.

Her tears flowed like a raging river, a catharsis not just for the current situation, but for every time she had been abandoned by those she had trusted. The memories came flooding back: the parents who never understood her, the friends who had turned their backs, and the lovers who had broken her heart. For what felt like hours, she remained there, kneeling on the cold forest floor, consumed by her grief.

She couldn't control her sobs, her entire being was wracked with sobs that shook her to her core. With her face buried in her hands, she felt utterly alone and forsaken. But then, amidst the pain and the darkness, she felt a warm touch on her arm. Slowly lifting her head, she looked to her side and saw the panther sitting next to her, its eyes full of compassion and concern. Its massive paws didn't feel threatening; rather, they felt gentle and comforting, as if to say, "I am here for you."

When the panther rested its paw gently on her arm, a sudden sense of calm enveloped her. The feeling of abandonment slowly dissipated, and she found solace in the presence of this new companion. With a heavy heart, she leaned into the panther, grateful for the warmth and comfort it provided in her time of need.

Gradually, her nerves settled, and she took a deep breath, focusing on regaining her composure. She reached for one of the bottles lying on the forest floor and took a few sips of water, wiping away the tears that still lingered on her cheeks. Sitting there in the midst of the mess her "friends" had left behind, she closed her eyes and took a moment to centre herself. "Get over it," she told herself firmly, determined to move past the hurt and betrayal she felt. After a while, she felt ready to leave, but before she could go, she knew she had to clean up the mess they had left behind. She was not only disappointed in her so-called friends for leaving her but she was also appalled by the litter they had carelessly strewn about.

Gathering the garbage, she felt a deep sense of disgust towards humans, wishing that she had never answered Mehul's call that fateful morning. However, as she sorted through the debris, she began to realize that some of the discarded items could still be useful. This thought humbled her, and she wondered how she could have ever been so wasteful back in the city.

Once she had finished clearing the space, she slung the backpack over her shoulder and turned to face the panther, who had been patiently watching her clean. The kind beast stared at her for a moment before standing on all fours and turning to lead the way out of the clearing. She followed, grateful for the panther's silent company.

Strolling through the woods, the panther occasionally stopped beside fruiting trees and turned to face her. Understanding the panther's nonverbal cues, she reached out and picked a few ripe fruits from the tree. As the juice dripped down her chin with each luscious bite, a fleeting respite washed over her, momentarily easing the internal pain inflicted by her friend's heart-wrenching betrayal. The taste of these jungle fruits was a revelation, an exquisite blend of sweetness and tang that danced upon her taste buds. With each succulent bite, she felt grateful for the abundance of nature's bounty.

She felt a growing sense of safety and security under the watchful presence of the panther, as they continued their journey. The prospect of surviving the night in the forest no longer felt like an insurmountable challenge. As the sun descended, casting long shadows through the dense foliage, they continued their search for a suitable place to rest. Her thoughts were consumed by the path ahead, the uncertainties that lay in the unknown. It dawned on her that no amount of careful planning could have truly prepared her for this arduous journey. A wistful smile tugged at her lips, for the very creature she had once feared as a threat had become her unwavering guardian in this labyrinth of wilderness.

When they approached the clearing, she couldn't help but feel a sense of unease. The silence was deafening, and the tall rubber and passion fruit trees looming over them only added to the eeriness. Stepping into the clearing, the dark beast settled itself on one side, succumbing to a deep slumber. Left alone, she stood there, her mind filled with uncertainty and indecision.

She scanned the area, searching for a suitable spot to retire to rest her weary bones.

As the temperature began to drop, her anxiety grew. The night was getting colder by the minute and she had no source of heat. She knew she had to try something to keep warm. With shaking hands, she began to gather twigs from the forest floor, her eyes scanning the area for any dry wood. She could feel the panther's eyes on her as she frantically worked, hoping to make a small bonfire. She struggled to get the twigs to light, her fingers numb from the cold. The panther opened one eye, observing her failed attempts. She could almost feel its amusement as it watched her struggle. But she refused to give up. She tried again and again, until finally, a small flame appeared. She let out a small cry of triumph and added more twigs to the fire. Soon, the flames grew larger, casting a warm glow over the clearing.

She sat back, feeling proud of herself but her triumph was short-lived when she realized the twigs she collected were damp, and the fire wouldn't be sustainable. She sat there staring at the smouldering fire, frustration building inside her. She turned to the panther, hoping for some encouragement, but it was sound asleep. She slowly made her way to the panther and settled in next to it. The panther's soft snoring provided a sense of comfort, and she decided to stay close to it for the night.

The next morning, Aaliyah was abruptly woken up by the sound of chirping birds and chattering monkeys. She groggily reached out and grabbed onto something soft and fleshy. Slowly, she became aware of her surroundings and realised that she was holding onto the panther's leg. She quickly let go and looked at it apologetically. It stared back at her with kind eyes, patiently waiting for her to let go. Her mind was still foggy from her peaceful slumber. She couldn't remember the last time she had slept so soundly. Sitting up and stretching she realised that the panther's warmth had given her more comfort than her fuzzy quilt back home ever could.

Despite the nightmares of the previous day, the tranquillity of the night had given her a newfound strength. While she watched the panther lazily wander around, Aaliyah felt a rare moment of peace. A few sips of water and some nuts and berries were enough to fuel her. But as her mind began to quiet, a new sense of anxiety crept in. How long could she really survive in the dense jungle like this without any supplies?

Watching the panther pace around the perimeter, she tried to think of a plan. Suddenly, the memory of a village they had passed on their way to the jungle came flooding back to her. Maybe there she could find help and make her way back to civilization. It was a slim hope, but it was better than sitting here, waiting for the worst. Thankful for the Portuguese she had learned in the last few weeks, she felt a glimmer of optimism. The pain and anger from her friends' betrayal still lingered within her, leaving her unsure about her feelings towards them. She realised that she needed to distance herself from them, and perhaps, she would call her parents for help. The mere thought of encountering her friends again made her stomach churn.

She was lost in thought, her mind racing with worries and fears. She stared blankly at the panther, unaware of the time passing by. But the panther was growing restless and let out a soft roar, shaking her out of her reverie. She quickly got up, realising she was still a captive and had to obey its commands. She folded her sheet and cleared the space of any human traces. Then, followed the panther out of the clearing, unsure of what was to come next.

They walked for what felt like hours, with Aaliyah lost in her thoughts and barely registering the changing sounds of the forest. When the panther finally stopped, she nearly walked into it, snapping back to reality. Looking up, she saw that they were standing in a quiet part of the forest, with a road visible in the distance. Her heart raced with excitement and fear. Was she at the edge of the jungle? Was she allowed to go? Could the panther read her mind? The emotions were overwhelming, and she felt like she was on a roller coaster.

She could see her freedom in sight, but something felt restricting about it. She felt a lump form in her throat, tears threatening to spill. She was surprised at herself for feeling bad about leaving the panther behind. There was something about its presence that had eased her anxieties, and she was once again becoming aware of the anxious lump in her chest. How was she not anxious while spending the night exposed to the jungle with a massive predator by her side?

Aaliyah's mind was a jumbled mess of emotions as she approached the edge of the forest. She couldn't believe that she was actually leaving the panther behind. It was as if a part of her was tethered to the jungle, and leaving it behind felt like leaving a part of herself behind. Staring at the road ahead, Aaliyah's heart was heavy with conflicting emotions. Although relieved to be returning to her comfortable city life, she couldn't help but feel a sense of inexplicable sadness at the thought of leaving behind the panther she had only met a day ago. She sat down on the forest floor, trying to find her centre amidst the chaos of her thoughts. "What is wrong with me?" she wondered. "I should be happy leaving this place."

She closed her eyes and focused on her breathing, trying to calm her racing thoughts. After a few moments, she got up with purpose, slung her bag over her shoulder, and thanked the panther for keeping her safe. Before stepping onto the road, she turned to bid her final farewell to the panther and found that it was gone. Upon realizing that once again she was truly alone in the jungle, her heart sank. Though her emotions threatened to overwhelm her, she reminded herself of the long journey ahead to find other humans. Taking a deep breath, she cautioned herself not to be foolish and that she must keep moving forward.

Aaliyah's mind was consumed with thoughts, and her emotions were fluctuating like the tides of an ocean. She hummed a tune, trying to distract herself from the overwhelming anxiety she felt. Walking down the quiet boulevard, she muttered to herself, "Maybe I should have stayed with the panther." The sound of her own voice echoed back at her, amplifying her doubts.

But her inner critic was quick to respond, "What's the matter with you? Stop being foolish and focus on getting to that village." The biting tone of her own thoughts only exacerbated her inner turmoil.

Suddenly, she heard a rustling sound behind her. She turned around to see a man walking towards her. She was relieved to see another human being after spending the night with a panther.

"Excuse me, do you know the way to the nearest village?" she asked, trying to hide the fear in her voice.

The man looked at her, sceptical at first, but then smiled. "Yes, I know the way. I can walk with you for some time."

She was taken aback when the man replied in English, but it was a pleasant surprise. As they made their way towards the village, they began sharing tales about their lives. Turns out, the man used to work as a guide at an Ayahuasca centre, helping tourists navigate their spiritual journeys. But he eventually decided to leave that behind and follow his true calling as a farmer. He wanted to devote more time to his family and reconnect with the natural world that he cherished. His face lit up as he talked about finding fulfilment in tending to his farm and embracing the wonders of nature.

She found herself opening up to him and sharing her own struggles. "I feel like I'm lost and don't know where to go," she said.

The man looked at her thoughtfully. "Sometimes, the best way to find yourself is to get lost," he said, offering her words of wisdom.

After walking for almost an hour, the man took a turn into the forest and bid her goodbye before disappearing into the dense forest.

While walking down the road, she couldn't help but feel bored and miss the chaotic sounds of the jungle, which had provided her with a sense of comfort. The realisation that she was alone heightened her anxiety and left her with an odd sensation.

"Why did I feel safer in the forest?" she wondered. "Why did I feel safe with that monster?" "What's wrong with me?"

Shaking off these thoughts, she tried to focus on finding her way back. "How can I find a phone in this jungle to call for help?" she pondered. Suddenly, she remembered her own phone and dug it out of her backpack. Unfortunately, it had no signal, and the battery was almost dead. "Useless," she grumbled.

She continued walking down the road, aware that she had the whole day ahead of her and confident that she would soon reach the village. Sauntering down the dirt road, she felt like she was transported back to her childhood when she used to stroll along the cement roads from school to her home in the army quarters.

Despite it being a pleasant day, she wasn't happy. She had won another trophy, which was now stuffed deep into her bag, but she wasn't looking forward to reaching her empty house with her lunch prepared and left on the kitchen counter.

Her brother had been away for almost two weeks, but she was happy that he was feeling better and would return from their grandparents' home soon. Upon entering her vacant apartment, she walked straight to her room, pulled out her trophy, and hid it deep inside her cupboard. No one cared about her accomplishments, and there was no one to celebrate her victory. She thought that she would show it to her brother when he returned, but he always told their parents about it, and then she had to go on a guilt trip. Perhaps it would be best to keep this one hidden. Despite knowing that her parents loved or cared for her, she still felt lonely.

As she cleared her table for homework time, she stumbled upon a copy of Harry Potter in her drawer. With some time to spare, she decided to bury herself in the wizarding world, where she could find comfort in the imaginary characters. At least they were always around, even if it was only inside a book, bringing her some joy and comfort.

Aaliyah's heart pounded in her chest as a single tear rolled down her cheek, blurring her vision. She quickly wiped it away, but the overwhelming emotion was too much to contain. "Why am I feeling like this all of a sudden?" she wondered, struggling to compose herself.

"Focus on the path ahead, Aaliyah. Don't be such an emotional fool," scolded her inner critic, urging her to keep moving. With a determined effort, she straightened up and focused on the road ahead when she heard a soft growl behind her. At first, she thought it was just her imagination, but the growl returned, louder and more aggressive this time. She froze in her tracks, sensing danger lurking nearby.

Slowly turning around, she saw three large, ferocious wild dogs staring at her, baring their sharp, menacing canines.

Escape

Her body froze, and her heart pounded so hard that she could hear it throbbing in her ears. The sound of the growling dogs sent adrenaline coursing through her veins, and her mind worked at lightning speed to find a way to outrun the vicious predators. As regret over leaving the safety of the forest crept up, she knew that escaping the wild beasts was her only priority. The dogs stood at a distance, giving her a head start. With a quick evaluation of her surroundings, she knew that running back into the forest was her only chance of survival. Her athletic memories from childhood flooded back, and she began the countdown.

Three... two... one...

Without a moment's hesitation, she turned towards the forest and darted inside. The growls echoed behind her, but the dense foliage helped keep her at a safe distance. This was the fastest she had ever run in her entire life, and her survival depended on it. The growls of the dogs gradually faded into the distance, but she refused to glance back. Going forward was her only option.

Despite the danger that followed her, the forest remained oblivious, and the birds continued to chirp and the monkeys to chatter. The adrenaline pumping through her veins made her immune to the stings and scratches from the trees and shrubbery that pulled at her pants and jacket. In the distance, she spotted a lone tree with a low-hanging branch. Her heart racing and her mind in overdrive, she summoned all the energy she had left and charged towards it.

The once deafening growls of the wild dogs were now mere whispers, but she dared not look back to see how far she was from her predators. With one swift leap, she landed on the foot of the tree and grasped the lowest branch to hoist herself up and away from the ground. But before she could even begin to pull herself up, she felt a searing pain shoot up her right calf.

She had been attacked.

Her survival instincts kicked in, and she used every ounce of strength to climb higher and higher, away from the ravenous beasts below. As she ascended, she could feel the air grow cooler and the ground seemed farther away. Finally, she found a safe spot to perch on a sturdy branch. She let out a deep breath, tears streaming down her face, as her heart continued to race like a thousand wild horses. The anxious lump in her throat made it hard to swallow or even breathe properly.

Regaining her composure, the barks of the wild dogs grew louder, but they were no longer a threat. They circled the base of the tree, jumping and howling furiously, trying to intimidate her. She sat there, proud of herself for surviving despite the pain and fear that were still coursing through her body. She looked down at her vicious attackers, with their teeth bared and saliva dripping from their muzzles, and smiled defiantly through her tears. But suddenly, a movement in the distance caught the attention of the wild dogs, and they darted off, their barks echoing through the forest. She watched them go, the adrenaline still coursing through her veins, grateful to have escaped with her life.

With the wild dogs now gone, she breathed a heavy sigh of relief, but her body immediately drew her attention to the next challenge. As the barks of predators faded away, she shifted her focus to her right calf and noticed a long, deep cut. Blood dripped onto the leaves below her, and the pain crept up on her like a merciless wave. Her smile turned into moans, and her tears became rivers. The forest echoed with her painful howls. With great effort, she lifted her right leg toward a nearby branch and tore a piece of cloth from her sheet. After pouring some water over the wound, she wrapped it tightly to stop the bleeding. Despite her best efforts, she could feel her energy draining. Straightening out her leg across the branch, she sat up against the rough bark, trying to control her tears. She took a few sips of water and pulled out a passion fruit and some nuts from her bag, slowly nibbling on them trying to distract herself from the pain. Eventually, her tears dried out, and she became numb to the pain. She focused her attention on the sounds around her and heard the low rumble of the clouds in the distance. The petrichor emanating from the grassy forest floor comforted her, and her mind wandered off to a faraway place, lost in her thoughts and memories.

"Mummmmaaaaa!" Aaliyah burst into the dimly lit drawing room, her voice echoing through the house, interrupting her dad's beer and the World Cup semi-finals on the TV.

Her mother rushed in, her eyes scanning Aaliyah's body for any signs of injury. "Oh my god, what happened?" she exclaimed, noticing the blood on her elbow.

"I fell off the tree," she muttered, tears streaming down her face.

"Be more careful, beta," her father remarked, briefly glancing at her before returning his attention to the television. Her mother hugged her tightly, guiding her to the dining table. "Drink this," she said, offering a glass of Glucon - D and wiping away her tears.

Sarthak, Aaliyah's brother, rushed into the room from his bedroom, concerned. "What happened, di?" he asked, looking at her with worry.

"I fell from the tree," she winced as her mother applied Dettol to the wound. Sarthak sat next to her, patting her leg gently, while her mother carefully dressed her wounds.

Aaliyah clung to the tree branch, shivering with cold and fear as the rain battered down on her relentlessly. The drops seeped through the canopy, drenching her clothes and making her feel as though she were slowly being submerged in a cold, wet world. Her mind raced with thoughts of escape and shelter, but her body refused to move. While she waited, she felt herself slipping into a kind of numbness, a feeling of detachment from the world around her. She longed to disappear into the tree itself, to become one with the bark and leaves, and never have to face the harsh reality of her situation again. But still, she clung on, holding out hope that the rain would eventually stop and she could find some way to survive.

Finally, as if in answer to her prayers, the rain began to ease up. She felt a surge of relief and gratitude as the clouds parted, and the moist air, warm and comforting, wrapped around her like a blanket. She closed her eyes and let the sensation seep into her, warming and drying her out. But even as she savoured the moment, a sense of helplessness crept over her. She realised that she was completely at the mercy of the forest, with no clear plan for how to escape or survive. She longed for someone, anyone, to come to her aid and help her find a way out of this precarious situation. She didn't want to die like this, alone and forgotten.

Lost in thought about her fate, a sudden muscle spasm jolted her and her grip on the branch slipped, causing her to cry out in shock and fear. Desperately, she clung on for dear life as the tree shook beneath her. For a fleeting moment, she thought she might plunge to her death, but by some stroke of luck, she managed to regain her grip and hold on. When the blood rushed back into her leg, the pain surged like a volcano. Every vein pulsated through her cold limb, and the wet cloth tied over the wound slowly turned scarlet. The acidity of the passion fruit in her mouth churned her stomach, and the oxygen burned her nostrils. Anticipating her body to succumb to the agony and embrace the worst, pearls of sweat rolled down her forehead.

Taking a few deep breaths, she carefully manoeuvred her good leg around the branch, allowing the blood to rush back into her leg until the blurs of green and brown faded away. With the pins and needles settling down, she cautiously placed her left foot on the branch below, avoiding any pressure on her right leg, but the searing pain made it difficult for her to concentrate on anything else. She carefully moved her left leg along the damp branches, gripping the bark as if her life depended on it. The last branch was three feet above the ground, and she had to jump to reach the forest floor. She sat on the final branch, preparing herself for the jump, but the slippery branch threw her off balance, and she slipped and fell directly onto the forest floor. Her hands cushioned her fall, and the grassy bed helped reduce the impact, but her wounded leg slammed against the foot of the tree, sending a sharp pain through her limb, which she could taste in her mouth.

She lay in the lap of nature, lifeless, staring at the life crawling on the forest bed, unaware of her torment. As her leg convulsed, she focused on the forest floor. She resigned herself to lying there, waiting for either a wild animal or the dogs to return and finish what they had started. Her body throbbed with pain, and she had nothing left in her to push through it. Her body, mind, and spirit were shattered.

Her thoughts were consumed by her parents, contemplating how they might react to her sudden disappearance. Would they blame her friends forever for taking her on this trip or leaving her behind? Could they ever forgive them for leaving her behind? The mere thought of Sarthak's devastation added to her anxiety.

Perhaps her friends had sent a rescue team to find her, or maybe her parents already knew she was lost in the forest. At least they would find her body unless some animal claimed it for their own. She couldn't help but wonder if predators preferred to work for their meals.

"Maybe I'll be useful for the scavengers," she thought.

"At the very least, I'll provide nourishment for the worms and flies," she thought grimly.

The forest was alive with energy following the rain, and everything looked stunning. It felt like she was living in a painting, and indeed, it was a breathtaking view to end her life. Birds soared overhead, and monkeys swayed through the trees, chattering away as if discussing the hapless creature on the forest floor. Breathing became a struggle for her, and her bag was drenched in sweat. Her blood pressure was dangerously low, and her eyes began to droop. She attempted to ignore the chaos of the forest and reflect on a happier time.

Her grandmother's gentle voice echoed in her mind, and she slowly closed her eyes. Memories flooded back to a time when she would visit her Amma during vacations. Her favourite moments were the times she spent on Amma's lap, with her long, frail fingers stroking her hair and singing her favourite lullaby. Amma's bony legs would poke at her skull, yet they would give her all the comfort in the world. She felt the hums in her heart and the strokes in her hair as she slowly drifted into numbness.

The warmth of the forest air embraced Aaliyah, recreating the warmth of her memories, and the forest seemed to sympathise with her. Tears streamed down her cheeks, leaving salty trails across her face, but her eyelids refused to open to face reality. The pain in her leg stubbornly refused to let her have any moments of peace, constantly demanding her attention.

As the forest grew quiet, she felt as though it was conspiring against her. The flutter of a pair of butterflies near her only added to her misery. She cursed the butterfly that had started it all, wishing she had slept through its loud flutter a few days ago. If she had, she could have been sipping cocktails with her friends in a cosy Brazilian bar or lounging in a hammock, lost in a good book, under the warm sun. Her mind raced with scenarios of what she could be doing if only she had chosen a different path, one that hadn't led to this moment. Each memory and possibility only served to add more tears to the already endless supply that streamed down her face.

She opened her eyes for a final glimpse of the magnificent forest, which she had hoped would provide a thrilling adventure but had ultimately turned into a harrowing ordeal. Her eyelids grew heavy, and her body began to slip into hibernation mode, with her heartbeat slowing down and her breathing becoming slower. Her eyes were closing, and her vision became blurred.

Waiting for her inevitable end, her eyes slowly blinked towards the dark abyss, fully succumbing to the darkness within. Just as the overwhelming void threatened to consume her, a familiar presence filled the air and a large, dark figure made its way towards her.

Revival

A frail, rhythmic pulse surged through her veins, as though her blood were dancing to a silent tune. Her body, once rigid and tense, now began to melt into the warm embrace of her surroundings. The darkness that had gripped her was slowly surrendering to the light of a new day, which emerged on the horizon like a glowing ember.

With every breath, her chest rose and fell, as though she were savouring the very essence of life. The sound of her own blood pulsing through her veins was like a symphony, a soothing melody that reminded her that she was alive. Laying there, she felt the cool, damp earth beneath her, gently cradling her back like a mother's embrace. Her wounded leg, once a source of agony, now found comfort in a familiar, warm touch.

A rush of energy coursed through her veins, enlivening every fibre of her being. She lay there, basking in the sensation of tingling warmth that spread from her toes to the tips of her fingers. The circulation had returned, and she could feel her body coming back to life, the strength slowly returning to her limbs. The forest around her slowly came alive with sound, with each leaf rustling and every bird calling out in its unique voice. The scent of fresh earth, damp and musky, filled her nostrils, reminding her of the raw beauty of the natural world.

The warmth of the sun, like a gentle kiss on her face, made her feel alive, while a soft breeze caressed her bosom, carrying with it the sweet fragrance of wildflowers.

Slowly, she opened her eyes, her gaze directed towards the canopy of trees towering overhead, allowing the gentle rays of sunlight to filter through. A nearby water body added to the symphony of nature, the sound of splashing water drawing her attention. Lacking the strength to sit up and survey her surroundings, she lay there, her vision blurry, staring at the trees above. Her memory was hazy, and she had no recollection of how she had arrived there. Everything was shrouded in mystery.

After lying there for a while, gathering her strength, slowly she raised her head. There it was, the dark, mysterious panther perched gracefully at her feet, with one large paw delicately holding down her wounded leg. Its sleek, glistening coat shone brilliantly in the sunlight, its eyes sparkling with an otherworldly glimmer.

While she gazed at the panther, she thought she saw a hint of a smile on its face, though she couldn't be sure if it was real or a result of her lingering dizziness. Turning her attention to her injured leg, she noticed that it was now covered in a curious paste, a strange mixture of purple and green. The pain had subsided, and she could feel her wound slowly healing as if the paste were imbued with some miraculous healing power.

With a slow and careful movement, she turned her head and gazed around, taking in her surroundings. To her surprise, she found her bag placed neatly beside her, and a bottle of water rested beside it, the droplets of condensation gleaming in the sunlight. The sight of the water made her parched throat scratch, and she longed to quench her thirst.

With a groan, she pushed herself up and sat upright, her eyes fixed on the bottle. As she reached for it, the panther sat up too, its eyes trained on her every movement. The intensity of its gaze conveyed a deep understanding between them as if they shared a connection beyond words. She twisted the cap and brought the bottle to her lips, the cool water washing down her throat and soothing her parched tongue. She savoured the sensation as the water flowed through her body, rejuvenating her senses and filling her with newfound vitality.

While she took in her surroundings, the panther strolled over to a nearby tree and returned, a small branch of ripe purple passion fruit dangling from its mouth. Weary but grateful, she managed a weak smile as the panther approached her, settling close to her wounded leg and gently placing its paw upon it. She sensed a sigh of contentment escaping the gentle giant as she reached out for the fruit.

The juicy flesh of the passion fruit proved to be an elixir, reviving her depleted energy and nourishing her starving body. She attempted to shift her wounded leg, but the panther's paw was firm as if to encourage her to rest and allow her wounds to heal. Yielding to its silent wishes, she reclined, feeling the comforting warmth of the panther's presence beside her. With each passing moment, her breathing became more rhythmic, and the knot of anxiety that had gripped her chest slowly unravelled. She felt secure and shielded in the panther's presence, reassured that she had conquered the worst and that it would remain by her side until she made a full recovery. Slowly, the tranquil sounds of the forest enveloped her, taking her back to a time when she had felt at home and at peace with the world. With her eyes closed, she drifted off into a peaceful slumber, feeling more at ease than she had in a long time.

Little 6-year-old Aaliyah bobbed her little head over the marigolds and the jasmine plants lined neatly along the boundary wall. The subtle fragrance of the marigolds and the jasmines permeated the pleasant, warm air of late February. Bees joyfully hovered around, collecting nectar and buzzing from one plant to another. For hours, she sat there watching the insects and birds go about their daily routines. She had become friends with them, and on weekend mornings, she would converse with them, sharing stories about school, friends, favourite foods, and her aspirations of becoming a storybook writer someday. The birds found comfort in her presence and would visit her every day, waiting for her to feed them the special seeds she had secretly taken from the kitchen.

Occasionally, Sarthak would join her, but his toddler energy often frightened the birds away. Aaliyah cherished her alone time in the garden, observing the life around her and confiding in her feathered friends. In that garden, she felt like herself and understood.

On a peaceful Sunday morning, she sat in the garden, happily chatting with her friends while her father sat on the porch, sipping his morning beverage and reading the newspaper. Suddenly, he called out to Aaliyah's mother, Reva, in a concerned tone. She was taken aback by her father's tone and turned to see her parents discussing something in a hushed manner, occasionally glancing over at her. Although she smiled at them, only her mother managed to return a weak smile, while her father's response was sombre. After a few minutes of what appeared to be a heated discussion, her father picked up his newspaper and angrily marched back into the house, slamming the door behind him.

Sitting on the porch steps, her mother motioned for her to come and sit next to her. Eagerly, she hopped over and took a seat beside her. "What happened, Mumma?" she asked in a gentle tone.

"Nothing, sweetie. What were you doing when your papa was with you?" her mother asked.

"I was talking to my friends,"

"What friends?"

"Mango, Bell, Honey, and Snow," she answered, a smile spreading across her face.

"Where are they now?" her mother asked with a hint of concern.

"They flew away when Papa called you," Aaliyah replied confidently. Her mother looked puzzled.

"Flew away?"

"Mango is a parrot, Bell and Honey are sparrows, and Snow is a pigeon," she explained while absently playing with the dirt on her toes.

"How do you talk to birds, Lali?" her mother asked, looking at her with amusement.

She shrugged and gazed up at her mother with an innocent expression.

"Aww, my sweet child, don't be silly. Birds can't understand us, and we can't talk to them," her mother chuckled, giving her a gentle hug.

"But they understand me," Aaliyah protested in her high-pitched voice.

"Okay, okay, you can talk to them when your papa is not around, alright?" her mother conceded.

"Why?" she inquired.

"Um, well, he doesn't quite understand your friendship with the birds. He thinks it's a bit odd," her mother explained while patting her back. She glanced at her feathered friend Mango, perched on a nearby branch, and replied, "Okay," in a despondent tone.

"Okay, come on, I'll make you a yummy sandwich, and then you can read a book inside," her mother offered.

"But I want to stay outside a little longer and play with my friends," she protested.

"You've played enough, Aaliyah. Let's go inside," her mother said, raising her voice slightly.

She stood up and glanced one last time at her friends, who were happily chirping away while feeding on seeds in the garden.

Overwhelmed by a tsunami of emotions, she burst into hysterical sobbing, but her inner critic didn't stop her from letting out her feelings. After a few minutes, she felt a warm breath on her neck and a cool, damp touch on her cheek. Opening her eyes, she saw the panther's face next to hers, staring at her with a concerned look. She wiped her tears as the panther pulled away. Despite trying to control her tears, she couldn't, and she continued to sob until she felt she was done. She calmed down and regained her composure, and felt as though a heavy weight had been lifted off her.

Wiping her tears she slowly sat up. Something changed within her, something was different. She took a sip of water, picked a passion fruit, and dug into its juicy flesh, relishing the taste. While watching a kingfisher swoop into the nearby lake, she said, "I don't know what's happening to me," turning her head towards the panther.

"All of this feels like a nightmare, but also like a lovely dream," she added. "I wish to go back to the city, but somehow I feel comforted in your presence. Am I going crazy?"

The panther gazed at her with its glassy green eyes and gently placed its paw on her hand, which was resting on her bag.

She asked, "Do you understand me? What is happening?" The panther just stared at her. She stared back, wondering if she could see a slight smile on its face.

"No, no, that's just silly. You can't be smiling at me," she protested.

The panther withdrew its paw and picked up some leaves beside her bag. Chewing on the leaves, it turned to her wounded leg and dropped a fresh batch of purplish-green juice over the injury. She felt an immediate burning sensation on her injury and tightly clasped the sheet on her bag. She let out an involuntary shriek, and the panther placed its paw on her leg to prevent her from moving. Her leg spasmed, and she writhed in pain for a few moments, but she eventually calmed down as the sting faded away. Her body pulled her back down, and she laid her head down to rest. She had had enough; her body and soul needed time to heal.

* * *

As the gentle rays of the sun fell on her face, she opened her eyes to see the beautiful panther lying gracefully beside her. Its leg resting on her foot, and its face just inches away from her own. Its soft fur and warmth felt like a large fluffy pillow, and she had to resist the urge to turn and snuggle into it.

"Morning," she said involuntarily.

The panther let out a deep breath and slowly moved away from her, standing up to stretch its elegant feline physique. She watched as it walked toward the lake to drink water. It crouched gracefully while quenching its thirst and suddenly leapt into the lake to grab a fish that was swimming nearby.

The forest looked radiant in the morning glow of the sun, with the forest life going about their morning duties.

She felt peaceful and stronger from within. With a slight movement, she tested her wounded leg and felt the pain had subsided significantly. Uncertain how long she had been resting, she decided she was strong enough to stand. With careful movements, she rose and the panther leapt towards her, but she assured him she could manage. It stood close enough to support her, yet far enough to allow her to stand on her own.

It took her some time, but she found her balance and stood upright, feeling as though she had been grounded for years. She stretched out her limbs and felt her stagnant energy flowing freely through her body. Slowly, with the panther shadowing her, she walked towards the lake and stopped at the edge. She gazed at the water and the monkeys playing on the opposite side of the lake and smiled contentedly. Looking down at her reflection, she saw a younger version of herself. Big glassy eyes, dishevelled hair, and flushed cheeks with all the passion fruit she had been consuming.

"Hi there," she smiled. A younger-looking Aaliyah smiled back at her. "You look cute," she told her.

Despite limping around for a while, her wound wasn't causing much trouble. Although she felt a slight sting each time she moved her right foot, the pain was tolerable enough for her to persist. However, when the panther emitted a gentle roar, she realised she may have been overexerting herself and decided to return to her spot. There, she sat beside a fresh batch of fruits and nuts that the panther had laid out for her. While she enjoyed her breakfast, the panther chewed on a tangerine-coloured flower and dripped its liquid onto her wound. Although it stung at first, the warmth of the liquid brought her comfort, and she resumed her focus on the delectable meal in front of her while admiring the toucans flying above the nearby lake.

"I haven't felt this peaceful in such a long time," Aaliyah remarked, taking in the serene surroundings. "What is it about this place?" she pondered, turning to the panther beside her. "And what is it about your presence?" She added, surprised by her lack of fear toward the panther. "I don't even feel like returning to the city now. I wish I could reside here permanently, with better sleeping arrangements and more diverse food options," she chuckled. The two of them spent the day lounging in the clearing, enjoying the tranquillity of their surroundings.

As the sun began to set, the panther stood up and started walking away. She looked at it perplexed, but it stopped and turned towards her. She comprehended its unspoken message and gathered her belongings, preparing to leave the clearing.

"Where are we going?" she inquired.

The panther proceeded forward, making its way slowly through the dense foliage, with Aaliyah following behind, struggling to keep up. While limping along, she accidentally stepped on some pebbles, causing her to lose balance. The panther quickly hopped over to her side, but she managed to regain her composure. However, before she could continue on, the panther blocked her path and turned around to face her.

"I can manage on my own," she insisted. But it remained firm and continued to obstruct her path. "I'm telling you, I can walk," she reiterated, trying to convince the animal. However, it persisted, and she eventually relented. "Alright, fine. Are you sure about this?" she asked approaching it. It stood there, waiting patiently for her to mount its back. With some hesitation, she slowly clambered onto its back, ready to proceed on their journey.

As they moved forward, she could feel the incredible strength of the panther's muscles as it glided gracefully through the foliage, seemingly unfazed by the additional weight of her 60-kilogram frame.

The sun slipped beyond the horizon, painting the sky with deep oranges and fiery reds as it disappeared from view. The onset of the night arrived quickly, and the darkness engulfed the forest. However, the absence of the moon was replaced by an awe-inspiring blanket of twinkling stars that illuminated the skies above. She was transfixed by the wondrous display of the heavenly bodies, unable to tear her gaze away from the celestial spectacle above. Despite their long trek through the forest, she wasn't concerned about their destination; she had complete faith in the panther's guidance and knew that she had nothing to fear.

After hours of wandering through the dense woods, they stumbled upon an unusual sight, a vast expanse of plains that seemed out of place amidst the core of the forest. Yet Aaliyah's attention remained focused on the shimmering sky above, awestruck by the sheer expanse of the starry canvas that stretched out before her. She gasped in disbelief as they moved through the open field, surrounded by a landscape that seemed to morph before her eyes. The shrubbery transformed into a towering grassland, with trees of different varieties dotting the horizon in the distance. While gazing up at the mesmerising sky, a colossal bird with luminous purple stripes soared overhead, stunning Aaliyah to silence.

"What on Earth was that?" She exclaimed in amazement, finally breaking her trance and looking down. Suddenly, she realised that they were in the middle of a surreal, otherworldly landscape that bore no resemblance to the Amazon.

Exposure

The duo was surrounded by lush, jade-coloured grass, adorned with delicate stripes of glittering gold. A subtle, sweet aroma of tangerine and mint wafted through the air, emanating from the tiny white and pink flowers that blossomed in the grass as they walked.

Aaliyah was mesmerised by the beautiful scenery and couldn't resist asking, "Where are we?"

A smooth, husky voice replied, "You'll know soon."

Confused, she looked around, trying to figure out who had spoken. But all she could hear was the rustling of the grass and the gentle hum of the breeze.

"Who was that?" she said, her voice tinged with uncertainty. For a moment, silence hung heavy in the air, and she couldn't help but wonder, "Am I hearing voices now?"

In response, the husky voice returned, "Yes, you are."

Panic crept into her tone as she asked, "Whose voice is this?"

"The one shadowing you for the last few days," came the answer.

"Wait, what?" she asked, leaning forward to get a better look at the panther. "How are you able to talk?"

"In order to hear everything, you must quiet your mind," replied the voice.

"That's not enough of an explanation," she protested.

"Take a deep breath and relax. You have too many questions. All will be revealed in due time," the voice advised.

She followed the voice's suggestion, taking a deep breath and focusing on the path ahead. They glided through the clearing, and the blades of glowing grass stretched out before them, leading to a heavily wooded area. The ground was blanketed with a fresh layer of white moss, soft and cushiony underfoot like a fresh snowfall in early winter. But as they stepped onto the mossy ground, it transformed before their eyes, shifting from a vibrant carmine hue to a deep, dark violet with every step. With each footfall, a trail of fragrant lavender was left behind. Aaliyah's eyes widened at the unusual sight, but the rapidly changing landscape captured her attention, overpowering her curiosity.

The trees that surrounded them were giants, standing tall and proud with emerald trunks that were adorned with intricate stripes of indigo and yellow, running from the ground all the way up to the branches. Every vein in the trees pulsed with life, gracefully carrying little bubbles of nutrients from the earth up to the leaves that rustled gently in the breeze. Aaliyah was bewildered when she gazed up at the luminescent veins, marvelling at the intricate web of life that surrounded her. Looking closer, she saw small creatures crawling along the branches, their fluorescent bodies glowing with a rainbow of colours while they fed on the leaves that danced in the gentle breeze at the edge of the branches. She squinted, trying to identify what kind of creatures they were, but was left baffled by the kaleidoscope of colours that emanated from their tiny bodies.

Enraptured, she watched as life crawled through the trees, and watched how each creature harmoniously connected to the others. The luminescence of the trees blended with the starry night sky, creating the illusion of them floating amongst the stars while they glided through the forest. A gentle warmth seemed to emanate from deep within her, spreading throughout her body like a cosy blanket on a cold winter night. It was as though the very essence of this magical place had seeped into her soul, filling her with an indescribable sense of contentment and peace.

Looking out at the stunning vista before her, a smile slowly crept across her face, transforming her features into a picture of pure, unadulterated joy. Her eyes sparkled with wonder and amazement, and she felt as though every worry, every care, had been swept away in the majesty of this moment. Her heart seemed to overflow with emotion, as though it could barely contain the sheer magnitude of the beauty that surrounded her. She felt as though she had been transported to another world, a place of pure magic and wonder, where anything was possible.

With glistening eyes, she whispered to her silent companion, "Thank you for bringing me here."

Moving deeper into the woods, unusual whispers filled the forest, gradually coalescing into a symphony of sounds that reverberated through every branch, leaf, and creature. The very forest itself seemed to dance to the rhythms of the symphony, breathing life into the sounds that echoed through the woods, enveloping them in a mystical aura. The wooded expanse gave way to a vast open space, and she was momentarily blinded by the intense glow emanating from the ground. She instinctively shielded her eyes with her hands as they moved closer to the source of the brilliant light.

"Open your eyes," requested the voice, and Aaliyah cautiously uncovered her eyes, unsure of what she would find. What greeted her was a breathtaking view of a fluorescent blue lake, glowing like a jewel in the moonless night beneath a canopy of sparkling stars. The panther came to a stop by the shore of the lake, and Aaliyah had a sudden sense of deja vu, though the overwhelming beauty of the location kept her attention fixed on the stunning sight before her.

"We will rest here for a while," he announced and she slowly dismounted from his back, limping towards the lake's edge. But before she could reach the shoreline to dip her toes into the cool, inviting waters, he intervened.

"Don't go there yet. Sit here," he instructed, walking over to the lake and dipping his muzzle into the water to drink.

She sat nearby, watching him with a blank expression, desperately hoping to glean some answers from him. Without warning, he turned and walked towards her, his movements slow and deliberate. He leaned down towards her wound and poured some of the glowing water over it, causing an intense, searing pain that shot up through her body and up to her temple. She gritted her teeth, fighting back the urge to scream, and instead focused on the dazzling arm of the galaxy that twinkled through the cosmic clouds overhead. Gradually, the pain began to subside, leaving her feeling dazed and confused. She wondered if she was dreaming or if she had died and somehow crossed over to another plane of existence.

"You're waking up," came the voice, startling her out of her thoughts.

"Can you read my thoughts?" Aaliyah asked, still struggling to process everything that had happened.

"As can you," he replied, and suddenly she realised that he wasn't exactly speaking to her. Instead, she had been reading his thoughts all along, ever since they had entered this strange and wondrous part of the forest.

"What is this place?" She inquired with wonder in her voice.

"This is the inner world of the forest," he replied. "Here, every being communicates through thought and energy."

She inspected her wound, only to discover that it was now fully healed, leaving behind only a small scar. "How did this heal so quickly?" she asked in amazement.

"This is our sacred lake," he explained. "Its water possesses healing powers."

She touched her once-injured skin but felt no sting or pain. She even shook her leg, expecting to feel a familiar ache, but it was nowhere to be found. Instead, she was overcome by an unfamiliar sense of emptiness.

He sat down next to her and offered some advice, "I understand that you have many questions. My suggestion is to take it one step at a time, and eventually, you will begin to understand everything." she nodded in agreement.

"Are there others like you in this place?" she inquired.

"No one is the same here. Each living entity is unique in appearance and purpose," he replied.

"Where do they reside?" she asked.

"Further inside,"

"Do you have a name?" she questioned.

"Yes,"

"What do they call you?"

"Sombra," he replied.

"That name seems to suit you well," She smiled. "How long have you lived here?"

"I've lived through many generations,"

"Will I ever leave this place?"

"That would be up to you," he answered, standing up to leave.

She stood and stretched, feeling the strength return to her wounded leg. She felt invigorated. She walked towards the lake and felt the urge to touch the glassy water. But Sombra stopped her, "Not yet. We'll return when you're ready."

Disappointed, she sighed and turned towards him. With each step she took, she could feel a faint vibration and hear a gentle beat. The colour of the ground changed under her feet. With every step she took, the ground turned from a pale yellow to a dull azure, leaving a mint trail behind her while Sombra's trail remained lavender.

"You'll find your answers soon," he said before she could even ask.

When they walked towards the orchard, she couldn't help but notice the tall, narrow trees with white trunks that had emerald-coloured veins running through them, extending up to the branches. The branches were adorned with bright orange fruits that swayed gently in the breeze.

They walked slowly through the orchard and soon enough, rays of light started filtering into the forest from a distance. Approaching closer, a warm breeze welcomed them, and the landscape slowly changed from tall trees to shorter ones, shrubs, and finally, short blades of coral grass. Although she wished to stay longer and observe life inside the woods, she was too curious about exploring other life in this mystical world. They continued on their journey, and she began to hear a new set of whispers. The rhythmic beats gradually turned into gentle, incomprehensible words. A moment later, a stunning child darted past them.

"Wait!" Aaliyah exclaimed. "Was that a child? Are there humans here?"

Before she could finish her thought, two more children pranced out from the other end of the grove. They were clad in airy white garments, and their skin resembled velvety rose petals. One child had aubergine-coloured skin and long, curly silver hair, while the other had peach-coloured skin and straight black hair. The children held hands, strolling in the same direction as Aaliyah and Sombra. Her eyes widened in disbelief as she observed their stunning appearance. The whispers around her grew louder and she noticed adults walking on the opposite side. Gradually, they entered what appeared to be a village, and her sense of wonder only grew. Walking deeper into the village, she couldn't help but marvel at the beauty of every resident she saw. They were like living works of art, each one crafted with utmost care and love.

A tall woman caught Aaliyah's attention. Her amber-coloured

skin glistened under the starlight and her long charcoal hair cascaded down her back like a waterfall. Watching her cradle her baby, she couldn't help but feel a rush of tenderness fill her heart. The woman's bright purple eyes sparkled with love and joy, radiating a warmth that enveloped the entire village. While she gawked at the mother and her child, a tall slender man walked past them, leaving behind an earthy fragrance that filled her nostrils with a heady scent. She turned towards him, her eyes searching for the source of the seductive aroma, and noticed his striking features. His dark blue skin gleamed, reflecting the soft glow of the night sky, while his long silver hair swayed gracefully with the gentle breeze. Aaliyah's gaze followed his to a breathtaking woman standing on the other side of the village. She was a vision to behold, with her lavender skin and long, wavy hair flowing to the ground like a serene river flowing into the ocean. Her beauty took Aaliyah's breath away, leaving her feeling both envious and in awe.

Her steps became slower as she continued to look around the village, her curiosity piqued like that of a young child in wonderland. Every resident she saw was a masterpiece in their own right, each one unique and captivating.

Moving deeper into the village, her attention was drawn to the sound of children's laughter. She turned to see a group of children playing with a giant russet bear, their carefree giggles ringing through the village like music. She couldn't help but smile at the sight, feeling a sense of joy and wonder that she hadn't experienced in a long time.

In the midst of all these ethereal beings in this inner world, she felt like an alien, but they didn't seem to mind her presence. She continued to stare at each new being that came into her view, while they went about their daily lives.

"Why does no one seem to mind my presence?" Aaliyah asked.

Sombra replied, "Do you want them to mind your presence?"

"I don't know," she hesitated.

"If you want them to, they will," Sombra said, and Aaliyah noticed a few villagers looking in her direction.

Quickly she shook her head and said, "No, I don't want to be a bother."

"Then focus on your path. Breathe, still your mind," Sombra instructed.

She took a deep breath and focused on the scent of musk and wet earth in the air. She let the natural fragrance fill her lungs and energise her body. As her attention returned to her own path she noticed that everyone around her was engrossed in their own actions and not bothered by her presence any more.

While following the lavender trail left by Sombra, she observed how the colours of the trail seeped into the earth, resembling flowing water. The ground appeared almost translucent as the energy generated by every creature that stepped on it moved rhythmically through hair-like veins into the glowing trees and plants lining the trail.

Engrossed in her observations, a sudden bright light caught her attention at the edge of her vision. Raising her head, she noticed a colossal tree on the horizon with a massive golden orb of light radiating from its base, illuminating the entire surrounding area.

On approaching the massive tree, the light emanating from it grew brighter, drawing many of the village residents towards it. She felt an eerie sense of tranquillity on getting closer to the mysterious energy, her steps becoming shorter and her breaths deeper. She sensed a strange shift within herself, as if the gravity had intensified, making it difficult for her to keep up with Sombra.

"I need to rest for a bit," she said, her energy depleted.

"Sure, we can stop here," he replied, leading her towards a nearby tree.

A little girl approached Aaliyah with a small vessel filled with a rust-coloured liquid, a smile on her face as she offered it to her. Grateful, she accepted the vessel from the girl's dainty pink fingers and thanked her with a smile. Taking a seat, she took a sip from the vessel and felt a sudden surge of energy. Grateful for the child's gesture, she silently blessed her with each sip. The child returned a warm smile while placing her hand on Aaliyah's face. Sombra sat beside her, gently resting his paw on her lap. She closed her eyes and focused on her breathing, gradually feeling warm, healing energies flowing into her from all directions. When she opened her eyes, she was astonished to see the villagers surrounding her, their hands placed on her body. Overwhelmed with love, tears streamed down her cheeks. Feeling strengthened and ready to move on, she thanked everyone as they dispersed in various directions, each with a smile. Waiting patiently, Sombra stood beside Aaliyah while she readied herself to resume their journey. With renewed strength, she stood up, eager to face whatever awaited them at the colossal tree.

Advancing towards the tree, she observed a subtle shift in the colour of her trail, and her steps became lighter. Despite her curiosity, the tree's pull was irresistible, and she followed without question. Upon reaching the tree, Sombra stopped and faced Aaliyah. "This is the heart of our village," he explained, his emerald gaze fixed on the massive tree. "It serves as our guiding light, the essence of our existence, and it provides everything we need for our journey." Aaliyah gazed at the shimmering core, feeling its intensity resonate in her heart.

"Approaching the core may feel overwhelming at first, but gradually you will feel at one with it," he cautioned, anticipating her unease. She nodded slowly, resolved to face whatever lay ahead. Sombra led the way as they approached the core.

The golden sphere rotated gently, its surface reflecting a delicate rainbow film in the surrounding light. She felt tears streaming down her face and her palms growing sweaty with nervousness. She placed a hand on Sombra, who slowed his pace to match hers. The intense radiance emanating from the core blinded Aaliyah, causing her to close her eyes and rely on Sombra to guide her forward. On their arrival, Sombra halted and announced,

"We have arrived."

With trepidation, she opened her eyes, and to her amazement, she beheld a wondrous sight.

Discovery

As she drew closer to the base of the enormous Ceibo tree, an overwhelming white glow engulfed her vision, illuminating the surrounding forest with its intense brilliance. She squinted her eyes and focused beyond the glow, and to her amazement, a human figure began to take shape.

Perched atop a rock, the source of the light emerged from the darkness of the forest. The figure was an embodiment of energy and light, with porcelain-white translucent skin that allowed strings of colourful energy to shine through. Her long, silvery hair cascaded down to the forest floor, like a fluid river teeming with butterflies, birds, and frogs that had peacefully made their homes upon the strands. Her translucent head shone with a violet hue, like the starry night sky radiating its energy through her hair, making it glow. Her large eyes were partially closed as if she were present in an alternate spiritual realm while being physically present in this mystical forest. Her omniscient smile was a reflection of her knowledge of the beyond, and it seemed to hold the secrets of creation itself. Wrapped in drapes of nettle and silk, she sat with her hands open to the cosmos, inviting the energy of the universe to flow through her.

Sombra and the other villagers moved closer to the ethereal being, drawn to her radiant love and wisdom. They sat around her in reverent silence, humbled by her presence. Touching her feet, kissing her hands, and absorbing her energy, joy and love illuminated their faces. Aaliyah's heart swelled with emotion, and tears streamed down her face as she beheld the otherworldly figure before her.

Overwhelmed, she collapsed to the ground, her heart aching with decades of pain that she had suppressed for so long. But as she surrendered to the catharsis, she felt a gentle lavender flower bloom in her mind's eye. Its petals opened one by one, revealing a brilliant orange core that sparkled with green and yellow spots. The flower's radiance filled her with an overwhelming feeling of love, washing over her and evoking a deep sense of compassion. Then, the ethereal being's long fingers ran through Aaliyah's hair, and a heavenly voice echoed through her body, commanding her to rise. With newfound strength and clarity, Aaliyah lifted her head, feeling a powerful connection to herself, the otherworldly being in front of her, and everything around her.

She lifted her head, feeling as though she was being lifted by a weightless force. Slowly sitting up, her eyes locked in with that of the celestial figure in front of her. The being's eyes were a deep, dark colour that seemed to absorb the light around them. And yet, amidst the darkness, there were tiny points of light that twinkled like stars. A golden ring encircled the pupils, and within the ring, a bright orange orb floated, radiating an intense heat that made it impossible to hold her gaze for more than a few seconds. She tore her eyes away and took a deep breath, feeling the tension slowly leave her body. Her hands loosened their grip on her knees and she allowed her head to fall forward, her chin touching her chest. While sitting in silence, the soft hum of nature surrounding her, she became aware of a peaceful sensation settling in her bones. The gentle rustling of the leaves and the distant chirping of birds carried her away from the worries of the world, and for a moment, she felt completely at ease.

"You are healing, you need to rest," the voice echoed through her body.

Sombra rose to his feet, his movements gentle and fluid. "Come," he said softly, beckoning Aaliya to follow him.

When she stood up, she felt lighter than before, as though the gravity of the Earth had weakened. Her body seemed to have shed a few kilos in a matter of minutes, and she felt as though she could float away like a feather in the breeze. With a smile on her face, she took a few steps back and turned to follow Sombra.

They walked away from the core and proceeded towards what appeared to be the residential area for the villagers. She watched as most of the residents disappeared into large berry bushes, leaving her confused. She turned to Sombra for an explanation.

"The sleeping arrangement here is much more comfortable," Sombra remarked as they made their way through the bushy village.

Moving towards the bushy residence, her eyes widened in amazement at the ethereal scene unfolding before her. The village was illuminated by a myriad of glowing orbs, each one emitting a soft, pulsing light that danced through the air like tiny fireflies. They floated effortlessly over the bushes and branches, casting a gentle glow on everything they touched. One of the orbs drifted toward Aaliyah, its shimmering surface revealing intricate patterns of glowing energy that flowed through it like a river. She reached out to touch it, and the orb changed colour from electric blue to vibrant pink, as if responding to her touch. She watched in wonder as it darted back into the air, leaving a trail of sparkling dust in its wake.

Aaliyah's eyes widened in wonder, "What are those things?" she asked Sombra, who turned to look at her with a curious expression.

"What do you see?" he inquired, and she pointed towards the orbs, "Those orbs floating around, don't you see them?" she asked, confused.

Sombra shook his head, "I haven't seen those in a long time," he said with a slight sigh.

"I don't understand, what are those things?" Aaliyah asked impatiently.

"Desires," Sombra responded while he continued to walk ahead, leaving Aaliyah behind for a moment who stopped to get a better look at the orbs. "But why can't you see them?" she called out after him.

"Because they are your own," he responded, turning around to face her. "Am I the only one who can see those orbs here?" she asked, perplexed.

"Every resident of this village will see different manifestations of their own desires," he explained.

"You said you haven't seen them in a long time, when did you stop seeing them?" she asked, intrigued.

"It took me many years, but they disappeared after several years of living here," he responded, his voice tinged with nostalgia.

"Don't you miss seeing them? They are so beautiful," Aaliyah inquired.

"Indeed they are," Sombra agreed. "I spent many days mesmerised by those beautiful orbs. But slowly I realised that their only purpose was to distract me from my purpose."

"But they are also illuminating the path ahead," Aaliyah protested.

"That's an illusion they create," Sombra warned. "They help guide your path at first, but slowly you get lost in their beauty, which is when they stray you away from your true path."

Observing the mesmerizing dance of the orbs, Aaliyah contemplated Sombra's revelation. She was not convinced how these harmless orbs could be a distraction. Moving forward, she remained entranced with the floating spectacle. Suddenly, she bumped into Sombra, who had come to a stop. Breaking out of her trance, she realised that they had arrived at their destination.

A massive red berry bush stood in front of them, and he walked into a narrow opening in its branches. She took a deep breath, closed her eyes and carefully stepped into the red berry bush. When she opened them, she was awestruck by the sight before her. A magnificent mud hut towered above her, surrounded by the vibrant red berries of the bush. A family of birds chirped happily from their nest atop the roof, adding to the hut's peaceful aura.

As Aaliyah approached the walls, she couldn't help but admire the beautiful hand-painted artwork that adorned them. The colours of red, purple, and green blended seamlessly together, radiating over the walls, telling the story of the hut's resident. Each painting seemed to revolve around Sombra, the master of this tranquil abode. Standing outside, Aaliyah found herself lost in the artwork and the expertly crafted windows.

Upon entering the hut, she was greeted by a large hall filled with handmade artefacts arranged neatly in the wall nooks. Plants and berries had crept in through the windows, adding splashes of green and red to the warm orange and brown tones of the interiors. While admiring the intricacies of the dwelling, she ran her fingers over the handcrafted pottery, baskets, and decorative masks. The vibrant shades of red, green, and yellow that adorned the walls caught her eye, and she took a moment to appreciate their beauty. She walked towards the window and noticed a cosy bed arranged next to it, made of soft nettle, delicate silk, and warm fur. She could feel the luxurious softness under her fingertips when she ran her hand over the bedspread.

"It's perfect," she said, turning to Sombra with a grateful smile.

As she lay on the bed, the fragrance of dewy grass and frangipani filled the air, and she was serenaded by the melodious chirps of birds outside the window. She quickly drifted into a peaceful sleep, her worries and anxieties melting away in the warm embrace of the bed.

The next morning, she found herself alone in the room, surrounded by the vibrant colours of the mud hut. While scanning the space, she noticed a beautifully arranged platter of berries and flowers on a large leaf, greeting her a few feet away from her bed. As she reached for the berries, Sombra walked in, and she greeted him with a smile. He nodded softly and smiled, his eyes lighting up.

"I'll take you around the village today."

She beamed with excitement, ready to explore the wonders of the mysterious village. She savoured her scrumptious breakfast, eager to begin her adventure in the enchanting village. She stepped out of the mud hut and was greeted by the golden rays of the morning sun which illuminated the walls with a soft glow. The birds perched atop the hut trilled a sweet melody, while the buzzing of bees filled the air.

Intrigued, she wandered towards the berry bush, its branches heavy with pink blossoms. The delicate petals were aglow with the vibrant hues of the rising sun, casting a warm light over the surrounding scenery. Standing on tiptoes, she inhaled deeply, taking in the fruity aromas of fresh strawberries and zesty lemongrass. The scents evoked fond memories of her childhood, of days spent exploring her parents' lush garden, surrounded by the buzzing of bees and the sweet fragrance of blooming flowers. Her heart overflowed with happiness, her eyes brimming with joy as she smiled at the bees buzzing around her. Suddenly, she felt a gentle nudge on her shoulder, and turning around, she saw Sombra gazing at her with amazement. Without thinking, she wrapped her arms around him and pressed her cheek against his velvety fur. It was softer than the finest wool and smoother than the finest silk she had ever touched. She savoured the moment, relishing the warm embrace, running her fingers through his fluffy neck, and caressing his plush ears. Her cheeks brushed against his whiskers as he nuzzled his face against her shoulder, breathing in the sweet scent of her hair. They stood there for a few precious moments, lost in the cosy hug. Finally, Aaliyah opened her eyes, stepping back with a soft smile on her face.

"Thank you," she said, her hand resting on Sombra's face. With a smile on his face, he led her out of their bush into the breathtaking new world of the village.

Following Sombra, she stepped into a bustling local bazaar where villagers exchanged artefacts, edibles, and small tools. The exchange process was fascinating to watch. The villagers would stop in front of each other, exchange their items, and then come close enough to touch their heads to each other before parting ways. The elders sat with the children, teaching them the art of crafting tools, jewellery, and garments, while adults roamed around exchanging goods for their everyday needs. While observing the busy scene, she walked up to Sombra with a curious expression on her face, but before she could ask anything, he responded.

"Our village thrives on a foundation of trust and honesty, and every resident works diligently to hone their unique skills. The village runs on this age-old barter system where the residents only take what they need, ensuring a fair exchange for all." Aaliyah observed the residents engaging in friendly transactions, exchanging goods that met their daily requirements. While strolling through the bazaar, a young man approached Aaliyah. She was instantly captivated by his musky scent and the sweet aroma of lemongrass emanating from his long purple hair. His flawless chocolate complexion glowed in the warm sunlight, and his perfectly chiselled jawline and sparkling ivory teeth were a sight to behold.

His eyes seemed familiar, but Aaliyah couldn't place them. Spellbound by his appearance, she wondered about the purpose of his approach. The young man gazed deeply into her eyes and then down at her neck. He noticed the black thread with the evil eye pendant wrapped securely around her neck, and his eyes widened in recognition. Suddenly, she remembered those eyes—they were Kartik's eyes. Removing the black thread necklace adorned with the evil eye pendant, the only keepsake remaining from their relationship, made her heart feel heavy. Trembling fingers held out the necklace to the young man, whose eyes mirrored the ones she had loved so deeply. With a weak smile and tears brimming in her eyes, she awaited his response. The man's gentle hands closed around the necklace, but instead of walking away, he pulled her into a deep embrace.

She buried her face into his chest, feeling the familiar grip from those years when she was with Kartik. She cried softly into his shoulder as the world around her faded away, lost in the memory of the man she had loved so much. After a few moments, the man released her, his lips pressing against her forehead—a gesture that Kartik had always made before leaving. Aaliyah watched as he disappeared into the crowd, and a part of her died with him. It was an unusual feeling, one of deep sorrow mixed with relief.

Silently standing and watching the villagers embrace each other and exchange goods, the negative feelings that had always lingered for Kartik finally faded away from her. She was left with a sense of acceptance and a newfound appreciation for the village's way of life. She turned to face Sombra, her eyes gleaming with unshed tears as she reminisced about the past. His curious gaze lingered on her face, taking in every nuance. With a wistful smile, she followed him out of the bazaar and into the outskirts of the village.

The eastern part of the settlement was an oasis of serenity, with tall grasses swaying in the breeze and a small pond that sparkled like a jewel in the sun. Drawing closer, she could see a small group of residents gathered around the pond, their faces serene as they meditated. Some of them had their eyes closed, while others gazed out at the water with peaceful expressions. The soft, lush grass beneath her offered a deep sense of calm. She lay down, closed her eyes, and breathed in the earthy scent of the soil. Sombra settled beside her, and she reached out to grasp his paw, feeling his warmth seeping into her bones. The gentle beat of the residents' hearts throbbed through the ground, and Aaliyah felt herself slipping into a trance-like state. The colours of the cerulean sky and the lush greenery surrounding her blurred together in a kaleidoscope of hues, and she felt a strange, unfamiliar feeling welling up within her.

Tranquillity.

It was a feeling she hadn't experienced in years, perhaps not since childhood. She felt tears prickling at the corners of her eyes as she savoured this moment of peace, a sense of homecoming that had been missing from her life for far too long.

Renewal

Enveloped in the cocoon of warmth, she observed as her exhaled breath wove life back into her physical being. Surrounded by the comforting warmth, she took a moment to reflect on her life. She realised that in her city life, she had grown accustomed to seeking out stress and anxiety. Instead of embracing tranquillity and stillness, she had become addicted to the rush of challenges and uncertainties. Living in the present moment had never been her forte. Instead, she was constantly plagued by the pains of the past and the uncertainties of the future, using them as a motivation to keep pushing forward. But now, as she focused on her inner world, the unfamiliar feeling of serenity began to unnerve her. It was a stark contrast to the constant chaos of her everyday life, where the bustle of the city was her constant companion.

For her, the city was a source of endless stimulation, a place where she could find new challenges and experiences around every corner. But in the process, she had lost sight of the value of peace and quiet, and the importance of taking time to reflect and rejuvenate. While she continued to explore the depths of her mind, she began to hear the distant melodies of gentle *icaros*, a reminder of the beauty and harmony that she had been missing in her city life. And for the first time in a long while, she realised the true meaning of tranquillity.

Struggling to embrace the peace that surrounded her, she tightened her grip on Sombra's paw. After a few moments in the tranquil state, she reluctantly opened her eyes and rose to rejoin the crowd. Glancing around, she found herself alone with Sombra, his eyes fixed on her. With a heavy heart, she began to make her way back to the bazaar.

"How do you live this kind of life?" she asked, her voice filled with curiosity.

"I don't know any other way," he responded with a calm tone, his words echoing in her mind.

"I am not used to this serenity, how do I deal with it?" she asked, her eyes searching for answers.

"When you stop fighting yourself, you'll begin to enjoy the peace within," he said, and his words hit her like a bullet. No one had ever called out her inner conflicts so openly. Her messy inside world was no longer a secret, and it was open for anyone and everyone in this forest to read.

"Don't you feel the need to have a secret world of your own inside?" she voiced her thoughts.

He smiled at her and asked, "Wouldn't it be easier to simply be truthful about what's inside of you with the outside world?"

Her mind struggled to comprehend his words, but deep down,

she knew he was speaking the truth. Her world was riddled with falsehoods, manipulation, and insincerity, and his world was the antithesis of that. The destructive behaviours she had endured and continued to carry with her were in conflict with the serenity that was beginning to settle within her veins. Her inner turmoil was overwhelming, and she collapsed to the ground to purge herself of it. Years of pain and toxicity were spilling out of her in the form of red and green liquids. Sombra stood by, waiting for her to finish. After wiping her mouth, she stood up once she was confident that the toxins were gone. She wiped away her tears with the back of her hands and continued walking back to the crowd.

"I know what you need," he said, taking the lead.

He led her through the village on a path she knew well, yet it appeared different in the daylight. The atmosphere was much more tranquil, with fewer people around. The sounds of the jungle reverberated through her body, creating a gentle hum that resonated through the forest floor. Nearing the source of the humming, Aaliyah's steps became shorter and uncertain and her breaths deeper. Sensing her hesitation, Sombra slowed down to follow her closely. The space was soon sprawling with residents, blocking their path, and Aaliyah's steps continued to shorten.

While she crawled through the throng, a captivating scene caught her eye. She paused to observe a young boy with an ash-grey snake, adorned with bright orange stripes, wrapped around his bare torso. She watched them intently relaxing under a passion fruit tree, basking in the golden radiance of the sun. Soon another boy joined the two and began playing with the snake. They peacefully played with the snake for a while, but suddenly the latter boy tried to take the snake away. The boys began to scuffle, and the snake managed to escape. This only escalated the situation, and their gentle tussle transformed into aggressive wrestling. She was taken aback by the sight before her, as she had never witnessed such behaviour in this peaceful village.

She watched in surprise as the young residents engaged in a fight, her eyes wide with fascination. After a few moments, she realised that some villagers were staring at her, and she noticed the gentle smile that had formed on her face as she watched the children scuffle. Sombra approached the children, and they quickly dispersed upon sensing his imposing presence. He turned to look at her, his expression blank as he walked slowly towards her.

"What happened to those boys? I thought fighting was not common here," she inquired curiously.

"We see what we want to see," he responded calmly.

Following Sombra, confusion clouded her mind. He was clearing the path for her, but she managed to stumble over a rock that seem to appear out of thin air. Falling to the ground, she clutched her injured toe, feeling the pulsating pain radiating through her body. As she sat there wincing, she noticed that the other villagers seemed unbothered by her distress, continuing to walk past her without so much as a second glance.

She couldn't understand their behaviour. It was in stark contrast to the night before when everyone had rushed to her aid. Now, they acted as if she were invisible. Sombra walked back towards her and gazed down at her while she massaged her throbbing toe. "Remove your hands," he said, and then placed his paw on her toe, causing her to wince. Despite the initial pain, the heat emanating from his paw felt therapeutic, and Aaliyah began to feel better within a few moments.

"Let's go to the lake," Sombra suggested.

"But I thought we were going to the source tree?" Aaliyah asked, feeling slightly relieved.

"We'll go there later," Sombra replied. While they walked away from the village, Aaliyah couldn't help but wonder about the strange behaviour of the residents. Before she could ask, Sombra offered an explanation.

"They change when we do. You only see what you feel inside."

"But I didn't want to see those boys fight or stumble upon that rock," Aaliyah protested.

Sombra was quiet for a moment before asking, "Are you sure?"

She wasn't entirely certain. A part of her didn't want to argue because she knew deep down, she didn't really want to visit the source tree. The silence between them was filled with the sounds of the forest as Aaliyah trailed behind Sombra, watching the colourful path he left behind. She observed little creatures scurrying along the trail while others worked tirelessly beneath the surface. She made an effort to avoid stepping on them, focusing on her steps. Why was she afraid to visit the source?

What was causing so much resistance today? Less than 24 hours ago, she had walked up to it with confidence, but now something inside made her hesitant to approach that powerful energy again.

"It's a journey, there's no right or wrong. Everything happens for a reason and in its own time. Relax your mind," his voice echoed in her mind, interrupting her thoughts.

As she was lost in introspection, she unexpectedly bumped into him upon their arrival at the lake. And there it was - the magnificent sapphire body of water reflecting the fluffy white clouds and towering trees. The lake was a true masterpiece of nature, nestled amidst the serene surroundings. Its shimmering, sapphire waters sparkled in the sunlight, emitting a radiant glow of ethereal energy. The air was filled with the soothing melody of the gentle ripples that cascaded across the surface, creating a mesmerising symphony that echoed through the dense foliage. Sombra approached the lake with a sense of reverence and sat down on the soft grass, carefully choosing a spot that wouldn't allow Aaliyah to see her reflection in the lake. Her heart racing with anticipation, she felt drawn towards the water like a moth to a flame. She yearned to feel the cool liquid on her skin, to immerse herself in the serenity that emanated from its depths.

But Sombra could sense her eagerness and cautioned her against it. "You're not ready yet," he said, his voice tinged with a hint of warning.

"Ready for what? It's just water, isn't it?" She asked.

"It's more than that."

She couldn't help but feel a twinge of disappointment. But she was in his world and wanted to respect the rules. Disheartened, she walked toward Sombra and settled slightly away from him. She gazed intently at the water, mesmerised by its ethereal beauty, twiddling a blade of grass at her feet while lost in thought.

While fiddling with the grass and the earth, her fingers found a small, flat rock, the perfect shape for skipping across the surface of the water. Memories of her childhood flooded back to her, of carefree days spent with her brother at her nani's home where they would have stone skipping competitions. With a deep breath and closed eyes, she reminisced about the simple joys of life. Running her fingers over the stone, she calculated the distance to the lake from her vantage point. Suddenly, a whiff of jasmine carried on the gentle breeze transported her back to her childhood, and without much thought, she stood up and flung the stone into the still waters. It skipped elegantly over the surface nearly ten times before disappearing into the depths, prompting an involuntary shriek of delight. She turned to Sombra for approval, but he blinked lazily, seemingly unimpressed by her achievement.

Undeterred, she eagerly collected more rocks and tossed them one after the other into the water. As the rocks ran out, the clearing came alive with the sounds of birds and insects, creating the feeling of an audience cheering her on with each successful skip. Overjoyed by her success, she hopped back to Sombra and settled down next to him, grinning from ear to ear. She instinctively slouched towards him, leaning her back against his muscular ribs. With each of his breaths, she felt as if she was being cradled like a baby. Basking in the warmth of the sun, she relaxed beside him and enjoyed the tranquillity that had returned to the clearing.

As dusk started to set in, she stood up and brushed the dirt off her back before declaring, "I'm ready."

Sombra stretched out his long, muscular limbs and rose to his feet. She took the lead and felt as if she was gliding through the trees. The space was surprisingly peaceful and empty, with only three or four villagers who seemed unperturbed by her presence. Crossing her path, the figures faded away as she hurried towards the source tree. The humming intensified, causing her fingers and toes to tingle with anticipation as they drew closer. Gazing into the distance, she noticed the absence of the large light bubble and caught a glimpse of the ethereal being she had encountered the night before from afar. Seated on the same rock as before, her eyes half-closed, humming with the wind.

"Guaia is the source of our energy and the spirit of our land," Sombra said.

A shiver ran down her spine as her response escaped her lips, "I feel that."

Guaia's porcelain skin and perfectly crafted features had Aaliyah completely captivated. After a few moments of staring at her, she asked, "Why do I feel so different in your presence today?"

Guaia smiled at Aaliyah's question and replied, "The closer you are to yourself, the closer you'll feel to me."

"How do I get closer to myself?" she asked, curious.

"You already have the answer to that; you practised it at the lake some time ago," Guaia responded with a gentle voice.

"By throwing stones?" she asked, slightly puzzled.

Guaia smiled once more and said, "Look below the surface, beyond the activity. How did it make you feel?"

Aaliyah turned towards Sombra, who was now peacefully snoozing with his head placed near Guaia's lap, and after thinking for a few moments, replied, "Excited, like a child."

Guaia sang, "That is a big step toward getting closer to yourself. Go deep inside, touch that child's heart, and feel how she feels." A knot immediately tightened around Aaliyah's chest, making it difficult to breathe as she tried to think about doing that.

"It's not easy," she mumbled.

"It can be as easy as taking a breath or as difficult as carving a mountain, the choice is yours," Guaia said with a soothing tone. Aaliyah wanted to say a lot, but she struggled to articulate her thoughts.

"Open your heart, my child. Bring peace and love to your world inside," Guaia said softly.

"How do I do that?" she asked, desperate for guidance.

"Swim through your depths, embrace the darkness, and follow the light," Guaia replied.

"What if the darkness consumes me?" she asked, fear creeping into her voice.

"It will only do what you imagine it will do to you. It can be your best friend or your worst enemy, the choice is always yours," Guaia reassured her.

"I don't think I have enough power to control my darkness," Aaliyah admitted.

"You don't have to control it, you have to embrace it," Guaia said with a wise smile.

"Why do I need to embrace the darkness?" she asked, still uncertain.

"Because only by embracing your darkness can you truly appreciate the light," Guaia replied, and with those words, Aaliyah felt a sense of calm enveloping her. "It's a part of you, my child. It's the yin to your yang, the moon to your sun, the light to your darkness. Without darkness, you cannot appreciate the light." she added

Aaliyah sat in contemplative silence, trying to understand Guaia's words. Sombra stirred beside her, sensing her confusion.

"But how do I recognize the darkness?" Aaliyah finally asked.

Guaia smiled gently and said, "Your heart will always know. Follow your intuition and trust in yourself. And remember, my child, that darkness is not something to fear, but rather a teacher. Embrace it, learn from it, and it will guide you towards the light."

She stared at Guaia, confusion dripping in her eyes. Guaia placed her hand on Aaliyah's heart centre and gently replied, "Close your eyes, travel back to your childhood, and think about your best memory. How does it feel?" she asked

Aaliyah did as she was told, and after a moment, she opened her eyes and said, "I don't know, happy maybe, or excited."

"Now, travel further back to a time in your childhood that you consider to be one of your worst days. How did you feel?" Guaia asked.

She felt an immediate rise in her heartbeat, her eyes filled up, her chest tightened, and she choked up. Her mind was flooded with all the unpleasant emotions she could think of, "Alone, disappointed, terrified, rejected, depressed, sad…" She couldn't hold back the lump in her throat anymore, and like a volcano, tears exploded through her eyes, consuming her in a cathartic frenzy.

"Without embracing the darkness, you'll never find the light," the celestial voice echoed through her foggy mind.

Guaia's hand on her heart felt like a bonfire in the dead of winter, slowly thawing her frozen heart. It was painful but comforting. As the knots began to unravel, the fog started to dissipate, and she began to see a warm light through the darkness that had consumed her all this time. The tears faded away, and she felt relieved of lifetimes of pain.

"Embrace your darkness, my child, for it is a part of you, just like the light. It is only through acceptance that you will find the peace and love you seek," Guaia said, with a smile that radiated warmth and wisdom. "The path can only be shown, but the walk is yours alone," echoed the angelic voice as the warm touch slowly retreated from Aaliyah's chest. She wiped away her tears and regained her composure.

"How do I...?" she pondered.

"Discover the love within, and your answers will reveal themselves," replied Guaia before returning to her spiritual realm.

Transformation

Aaliyah reflected on her conversation with Guaia as her eyes trailed the channels of light, creating an illuminated web in the canopy towering over her. She felt as though she had finally woken up to the realities of her life. For years, she had been seeing her life through a blurry lens, unable to truly understand her own situation. But now, everything she had ever known appeared to have a different meaning. She felt like she was now viewing her life as a bystander and was able to look at everything with a fresh pair of eyes.

She had been living her life as a victim of her circumstances, and now she felt liberated knowing that she was the director of her own life story. She had always been the driver of her life and had given away the steering to others, which made her feel like an outsider in her own life. She couldn't help but smile as she recalled all the times she had cursed and blamed those around her for her miserable conditions. While thinking about her childhood and all the times she blamed her parents for not being the people she hoped them to be, she realised that they too were living their own lives as outsiders. Even Kartik, her first love and one of the biggest mistakes of her life, was a reflection of herself in a different form. Every character in her life was a projection of her internal state, and it was all so obvious now. She likened this realisation to an illusionary painting, where hidden art becomes visible once seen, and cannot be unseen. The forest around her seemed to glow even brighter, as though celebrating this newfound realisation.

Her mind wandered through the memories of her past, playing back to the people and situations that she had encountered over the years. As she reflected on what she had considered pivotal moments in her life, she was struck by how they all related to her own internal struggles. It was amusing to her now that she had spent so much time seeking external solutions to her problems when the answers had been within her all along.

Lost in her musings, she began to giggle, and the sound echoed through the forest around her. She felt a warm and fuzzy energy radiating from within her, filling her with a sense of joy that she hadn't felt in years. Her laughter was pure and honest, and it reminded her of the carefree days of her childhood when she would chat with her feathered friends in the garden of her family home. As tears of joy streamed down her face, she felt as though she were floating over the soft, grassy forest floor. She felt a deep connection to the leaves that danced on the branches overhead and to the earth beneath her feet. It was then that she felt a tickle on her toes, and she looked down at her feet to see Sombra rubbing his whiskers against her bare skin.

"Hey, hey, stop it, that tickles," she exclaimed, giggling even harder as Sombra continued to brush his soft fur against her feet. She scrambled up to her feet and ran toward the open grasslands, where white blossoms sprawled across the field, as he chased her playfully. They both tumbled and played in the grass, forgetting their differences in size and weight as they frolicked together. The white blossoms around them emanated a sweet and minty fragrance, filling the air with a sense of purity and renewal. The forest rejoiced in their youthful frolics while the birds chirped and the bees buzzed through the fields.

As the sun began its descent, Sombra rose to his feet and walked away from the clearing. Aaliyah knew exactly where he was leading her, and she jumped up to follow him eagerly, "You think I'm ready?" Sombra turned to her and smiled, then continued walking.

While walking through the orchard of tall white and emerald trees, she noticed that the colour of her trail had changed. It was now a bright green, tinged with hints of blue and purple.

"What do these mean?" she asked.

"The colours reflect your internal state," he explained. "The colours that you see are the colours of your energy centres that are most active or the ones that need healing. When they are bright and glowing, it means you're healing those energy centres, while the dull colours indicate those that need attention and healing."

"What does green symbolise?" she asked.

"Green represents the connection with your heart, your inner self; blue represents the connection with your intuition; and purple represents the connection with the divine." Curious and fascinated, she gazed at the new colours that now followed her around. She leapt over the roots that sprouted over the ground and ran around the trees like an innocent child running away from an invisible playmate.

The night sky was their guide, dazzling with innumerable stars as the moon rose in the distance. The buzzing of the insects was settling down when they approached the healing lake. The warm blue lake welcomed them, and the fluorescent green trees decorated the clearing for Aaliyah's big night. Her excitement grew upon approaching the healing lake, eager to experience what was in store. Despite her attempts to learn more from Sombra's thoughts, she found his mind as still as the lake itself.

"Go ahead, you can walk into the lake," he said. "You'll need to step into the lake in your most natural form, without any clothes," he added.

She felt a little hesitant at first, this was the first time she would be naked in front of Sombra. "He's always naked in front of me, how does it matter?" she consoled herself and quickly stripped away her grimy, worn-out jungle clothes.

She had the urge to jump into the lake, but with the flutter in her stomach, she decided to approach the lake carefully. A gentle warm breeze greeted her, and she noticed the overwhelming reflection of the starry night sky on the still blue surface. It was like walking into the cosmos.

As she dipped her toes into the lake, she felt a warm tingle rising from her toes, spreading up through her legs. The water felt dense, yet fluffy as if she were stepping into a pool of jelly-like cotton candy. As she stepped further into the lake, she felt a surge of healing energy rising from her feet, moving up to her temple. She could feel every nerve end, every vein, and every organ inside her body tingling with the warmth of the water and the nurturing energy that was quickly engulfing her insides. She walked to the centre of the lake with the water covering her body up to her chest, and she turned around to look at Sombra. He was gone, and she was left alone in solitude to experience this all by herself. The forest was still and soundless, almost as if time had stopped for her. She closed her eyes, took a long, deep breath, and dipped her head in the water. A warm, fluffy cloud enveloped her crown, and slowly she opened her eyes to a view that was unbelievable.

She was amidst a bright blue energy web pulsating through her body. Integrated within this energy network, every nerve and vein in her body was glowing through her skin, flowing synchronistically with the energy pulsating outside. She could hear her heart beating through the entire lake, and she could taste her breath through the viscous water. She focused on the energy pulsating through the illuminated web, and slowly there was absolute stillness.

She was in a vacuum of peace.

Her body, mind and soul were all one with her surroundings. She couldn't distinguish the boundaries between herself and the energy that floated around her. She was one with the lake, the forest, and the cosmos above. She floated within this lattice for what felt like hours and was slowly pushed toward the surface when it was time for her to emerge into her revitalised form. Standing on her legs, she felt a newfound strength. The mushy lake bed supported her as she gazed at the thicket of pale white trees, the only witnesses to her transformation. The stars overhead twinkled brighter over the surface of the dark blue lake, which was now glowing around her body. Her body continued to glow with the connection to the network beneath the surface. She lifted her hands to find them looking paler than before, almost translucent, with her veins glowing through her porcelain skin.

While scanning the field, trying to locate Sombra, she noticed a dark figure standing at the edge of the clearing, staring at her. She tried to focus her vision to identify who it was, but the figure was standing far away, blending with the darkness behind. She looked down at the water to see if her vision was clear and was overwhelmed by the stunning face that looked back at her. The eyes twinkled like the stars, and the skin was smooth and glowing like the moon at the horizon. Transfixed by her own reflection, she forgot about the dark figure that was staring at her from a distance. She touched her cheek to make sure that she was looking at her own reflection and that it wasn't someone else she was seeing in the lake, and was overwhelmed when the reflection mirrored everything she was doing.

Why did this feel so familiar? She had never had an experience like that in her life before. She wondered if it was deja vu. And then, like a bolt of lightning, it struck her, and she was immediately transported back to a night a few weeks ago when she had seen a similar lake. It was the night of her Ayahuasca trip. She saw herself in the lake that night. Mama Aya had led her to this lake during her ayahuasca experience. She recalled the vision she had of herself when she saw a dark figure looking back at her in her own reflection. She wasn't that dark reflection any more. She smiled and hugged herself.

Turning her gaze towards the dark shadow at the edge of the

forest, a different figure caught her eye—one that she had been longing to see. She couldn't tell how much time had passed while she was in the lake, but being away from Sombra for even those few moments felt like an eternity. She walked toward him, smiling, and noticed a pile of white clothing that was placed neatly near the edge of the lake. The dress shimmered in the starlight, its soft fabric appearing almost weightless. As Aaliyah stepped out of the water, her body dried up almost instantaneously, and the lake returned to a state of stillness as her last toe pulled out of the viscous water.

With a sense of calmness and serenity, she gently picked up the beautiful white nettle and cotton dress from the ground, admiring the intricate details of the fabric. As she wrapped the dress around her porcelain skin, she felt a sense of purity and renewal.

"Thank you, for everything," she said, turning towards Sombra and embracing him in a tight grip. They stood there, enveloped in each other's embrace under the twinkling starlight. The trees around them watched silently as the ground glowed a bright green, illuminating the entire forest.

Initiation

Under the radiant moonlight, she gazed at the shimmering water, and the beautiful doe-shaped eyes blinked gently at her. It had been a few days, but Aaliyah was unable to get over her new appearance. It was the face she had grown up with for 20-something years, but somehow it felt like she had been seeing herself through many masks, which were peeled off her skin when she dipped into the holy lake. She threw stones into the water, trying to see if her reflection would change every time she disturbed the water, but the reflection was there to stay. She felt a gentle tug at the edge of her robes and saw Sombra pulling her off the edge. It was time to go to the village for the festivities.

As they entered the gathering of residents settled around the source tree, silence pervaded the air, but the excitement was palpable. She felt overwhelmed by the attendance at her party, and she glided slowly through the vibrant crowd towards Guaia. The colourful globules drifted around, casting a rainbow of hues in the sacred space of the bustling forest. Everyone was elated about her transformation. After spending a few days recovering from her metamorphosis, she was finally interacting with the residents as her new self. She was being initiated into her new life with the blessings and support of Guaia and the villagers.

Approaching the holy Ceibo tree, she sat at Guaia's feet with a smile, which was warmly returned. Suddenly, the energy of the space felt serene and she felt connected to everyone around her without being overwhelmed. She sensed that everything and everyone was an extension of her own body, and she could feel the energy of all the creatures pulsing through her from the base of her body to the top of her temple.

As Guaia placed her slender hands on Aaliyah's head, she closed her eyes and immediately saw the entire forest as a web of energy connected through hair-like energy strings. There were no forms or colours—just pure white energy connecting everything. Aaliyah could sense the gentle pulsating of the ground underneath her, as well as the heartbeat of the creatures residing in the trees. A new meaning of life and connectedness emerged for her as she explored the web through her new sight.

As she explored her new world, the residents hummed to the rhythmic beat pulsating through the forest. The session lasted a few minutes before a kaleidoscope of luminous butterflies floated into the gathering from the source tree, which was now glowing a bright green. Fluttering around her for a few moments, the butterflies settled all over her body, making her feel feather-light as a cool breeze surrounded her in the vortex of transformation. After a few moments, the butterflies launched back into the source tree, leaving her porcelain-like skin adorned with radiant green spots.

"You have entered your new life," said Guaia, removing her hand from Aaliyah's temple. When she opened her eyes, she saw the forest revelling in the initiation of her new life.

After the ceremony, an elaborate feast of scrumptious food was laid out by the villagers in the biggest potluck party she had ever experienced. Walking around and meeting the villagers, she thanked every resident for their presence in her life and for being there for her ceremony. She meandered through the bustling crowd, her eyes scanning the surroundings for something that caught her attention.

Turning a corner, an elderly couple seated beside a passion fruit tree caught her attention, their eyes fixed on her from a distance. She felt a mysterious force beckoning her towards them, and as she drew closer, a familiar aroma filled her senses - smoky musk and minty jasmine. It was a fragrance that transported her back to her childhood, evoking memories of carefree days spent playing in the garden. The scent hung in the air, wafting gently towards her as if carried on the breeze.

The man smiled warmly at her, his wrinkled face exuding kindness, and he extended his hand in welcome. She took his hand, and a wave of warmth spread through her body, causing her to feel a sudden sense of belonging. It was a feeling she had yearned for, one that had eluded her for the better part of her life. As she sat with them, she felt a tranquil sensation enveloping her. The man pulled her into a warm embrace, and she found herself resting her head on his chest, feeling a sense of safety and comfort she had not experienced before. The man cradled her while his partner hugged her from the side, evoking memories of her infancy. "I forgive you" she whispered instinctively as she gently wept into the man's broad chest.

At that moment, nothing else mattered. The festive celebrations taking place in the background faded into insignificance as she basked in the warmth and love of the couple. It was a warmth that she had yearned for since her childhood, a warmth that filled the void inside her. She wished to spend the entire night basking in the love and kindness of the couple, but a young girl hopped to pull her away, insisting that she join the celebration. Reluctantly, Aaliyah turned to face the couple, her eyes beseeching them to let her stay. The man pressed a kiss to her cheek, while his partner placed a tender peck on her nose, evoking memories of the tenderness her mother used to show. Overwhelmed with emotion, she succumbed to the little girl's tug and observed as the couple remained seated near the tree, gazing at her with adoring eyes as she was swept up in the crowd's embrace.

She was the life of the party, captivating everyone's attention. The residents clamoured to dance with her, offering her food, hugs, and kisses, lavishing her with all the affection they could muster. She had never experienced such intense affection before. She frolicked from one corner of the gathering to the next, forging new friendships, communicating with various creatures, and relishing the forest's finest produce. This celebration was a once-in-a-lifetime experience, replete with the sounds of drums, the forest's melody, and the joyous laughter of its inhabitants. The beat of the drums pulsed through her body, urging her to move with the rhythm. The symphony of the forest surrounded her, enveloping her in its tranquil melody, while the joyous peals of laughter filled her heart with warmth. She closed her eyes and lost herself in the moment. The memories came flooding back like a rushing river, carrying her away on a journey through time. Suddenly, she was no longer a grown-up burdened with responsibilities but a carefree child, twirling and dancing to her heart's content.

The joyous sound of her laughter filled the air as she spun and leapt, her arms outstretched as if she were trying to capture the very essence of happiness. She felt the wind rushing past her, lifting her dress and tousling her hair, but she didn't care. She was free. The world around her disappeared, and all that existed was the rhythm of the music and the beat of her heart. She closed her eyes and let the melody guide her movements, lost in the moment and the memories. She was transported back to a time when the biggest worry in her life was whether she had enough time to play before dinner.

As the music faded away, and the memories slowly retreated, she opened her eyes and found herself back in the present, but with a renewed sense of joy and contentment. She knew that no matter how challenging life could be, she could always revisit those carefree childhood days with a simple dance.

As the night wore on, she knew that this moment was fleeting. She looked around the clearing, savouring the sight of all the happy faces, the flicker of the fireflies, and the beauty of the forest. Amidst the festive revelry, the residents of the mystical village danced and sang, their joyous laughter filling the warm, humid air. In stark contrast, Guaia sat peacefully at her shrine, surrounded by the lush greenery of the forest, with her faithful companion Sombra by her side.

Feeling overwhelmed by the energy of the celebration, Aaliyah sought solace in their company and left the party to approach them. Sombra, sensing her presence, turned to greet her with his kind, gentle eyes. She was immediately overcome with emotion and pressed her temple against his, feeling the softness of his fur against her skin. She wrapped her arms around him, feeling his warmth and love enveloping her. The embrace filled her with an overwhelming sense of love and gratitude for Sombra, who had been her pillar of strength during her time in the Amazon. She felt incredibly lucky to have found such a loyal companion amid her struggles. After a few moments of intimacy, Sombra stepped back, leaving her to take a seat beside Guaia. Overwhelmed by her emotions, she spoke with a trembling voice.

"I feel so blessed," she said, with tears streaming down her face.

"You deserve every bit of it," replied Guaia with a smile.

"I wish I could have experienced this kind of life before," Aaliyah said.

"This life has always been within you," Guaia said gently. "You need only look deep within to find this love and joy."

"But it wouldn't have happened if I hadn't come here and met Sombra," Aaliyah said, her voice thick with emotion.

"Your choices led you to this place, Sombra was only a guide."

Aaliyah thought for a moment before asking, "How can I live this life in the city?"

"The world you see now is within you," Guaia explained. "And wherever you go, you take this world with you."

Aaliyah nodded thoughtfully, feeling a newfound sense of hope. "Can I live in this world and still live the life I had back home?"

she asked.

"Your definition of home will help you decide where you want to stay," Guaia said. "This world is a crossroads that will help you find your true sanctuary."

"I love my life here, and I love Sombra, but I also have a life back in India, where my family and friends are. Is it possible to balance both worlds?" Aaliyah asked, with uncertainty in her voice.

"It may be difficult to find your way back here as you leave, but this world will always live inside you."

Aaliyah took a deep breath before speaking again. "I want to see my family and friends, but my feelings for Sombra keep me from leaving. I don't understand my love for him. We're different species, but the love I feel for him surpasses any definition of love I've ever experienced. I feel like I'm fated to be with him, but how can I live a full life with him in this form?"

"True love transcends form and time," Guaia said with a reassuring smile. "But if your definition of love requires you both to be in the same form, then I can help you with that."

Aaliyah's eyes widened with hope. "How?" she asked urgently.

"I can turn you into the same form as Sombra, and you can live with him here for as long as you both live, or I can turn him into your form. But there is one condition," Guaia said gravely.

"What condition?" Aaliyah asked, her heart racing with anticipation.

"He will be turned into your form for one entire day. After that, you will have to leave the forest forever," Guaia explained, her tone sombre.

Choice

Guaia's words struck her like an icy breeze on a bone-chilling winter night. A sharp shiver ran down her spine, even though the warm summer air enveloped her. In a flash, she played out both scenarios in her mind, weighing the sacrifices she would have to make in either case. Her thoughts became tangled, and she felt overwhelmed by the magnitude of the decision. She stood there, motionless, for what felt like an eternity as she struggled to articulate her thoughts. "I…." Guaia interrupted her before she could respond, "It is not an easy decision, and you don't have to decide anything right now. Take your time to think about it, and tell me when you are ready."

As Guaia retreated into her spiritual realm, Aaliyah found herself grappling with the moral dilemma before her. Her mind was racing with questions, and her heart felt heavy with the weight of her decision. Despite her inner turmoil, she tried to push her thoughts aside and enjoy the rest of the evening. The party was slowly winding down, and the crowded clearing was rapidly beginning to empty. Amongst the dwindling crowd, she spotted Sombra, patiently waiting for her. Her footsteps were slow and hesitant as she made her way towards Sombra, her mind still reeling from the weight of the decision she had to make. The warmth of the summer air and the fading light of the evening did little to ease her inner turmoil.

Her steps gradually slowed to a measured pace as they started their journey back to their humble hutment. She took in her surroundings, barely registering the beautiful scenery around her. Her mind was consumed by the weight of the decision she was facing, and she struggled to process the gravity of its potential consequences. The beauty of the forest, once a source of comfort and joy, now seemed to mock her with its serenity. Her thoughts swirled around her like a whirlpool, and she struggled to keep her head above water. She felt a sense of overwhelming pressure bearing down on her, threatening to drag her under. Lost in her own thoughts, Aaliyah was suddenly brought back to reality by a gentle chuckle. Startled, she turned towards Sombra, whose bright eyes shone as he gazed at the illuminated path before them. The white pathway reflected the glorious moonlight, and the trees around them rustled softly in the breeze.

Feeling the weight of the decision on her shoulders, she asked, "How can you be so calm when you know exactly what I'm going through?"

Sombra's smile only grew wider as he replied, "Because, right now, I'm enjoying your company and focusing on the radiant path ahead of us. For me, this is all that matters right now." His calmness was infectious, and all her thoughts faded away. She wanted to embrace every moment with him now that she knew that, in one scenario, her time with him was limited.

* * *

Lying on the soft bedding, her eyes closed, she breathed in the mouth-watering aroma of freshly cooked curry leaves. The tantalising scent filled her nostrils, tickling her senses and making her stomach grumble with hunger. She heard the cricket match playing on the television in the background, but she paid it no mind. She was lost in her own thoughts, relishing the rare moment of peace and quiet with her father. She felt his warm hand stroking her hair, sending shivers down her spine. She smiled contentedly, savouring the moment, not wanting it to end. She knew her mother was in the kitchen, preparing breakfast, and her stomach growled again, urging her to get up and eat. But she didn't want to ruin this perfect moment with her father. She decided to feign sleep, hoping her mother would leave her alone for a while longer.

Suddenly, her mother's voice shattered the peacefulness, calling out her name. Aaliyah groaned inwardly, annoyed that the moment was being interrupted. She reluctantly opened her eyes, staring blankly at the TV screen, pretending to have just woken up. Her father, sensing her frustration, spoke up. "Go beta, go eat something," he said lovingly, his voice melting her insides. She hesitated for a moment, torn between her hunger and the desire to stay with her father. But the warmth in his tone urged her to get up and go to the kitchen.

As she entered the kitchen, her senses were overwhelmed by the mouth-watering aroma of freshly cooked idlis. She saw her favourite foods lined up on the counter, making her stomach rumble even louder. And then, she noticed a huge chocolate cake on the breakfast table with her name written on it with colourful gems.

"Happy birthday, my baby!" her mother exclaimed, hugging her tightly. Aaliyah's heart swelled with love and gratitude, feeling lucky to have such a caring mother. And then she heard her younger brother's voice, screaming "Happy birthday, diiiiiiiii!" as he ran into the kitchen wearing his Bugs Bunny pyjamas. She hugged him tightly, feeling overwhelmed with happiness and love for her family. This was the most precious gift she could ask for on her birthday—a joyful day with her family at home.

As Aaliyah blew out the candles on her birthday cake, she watched with delight as her family gathered around her, singing 'Happy Birthday.' Their smiling faces and the sound of their laughter filled the room, making her heart swell with joy. The warmth of the moment enveloped her like a cosy blanket, and she closed her eyes to soak it all in.

Suddenly, the sound of rustling leaves disrupted her peaceful reverie. Aaliyah opened her eyes to see a pair of bright blue macaws flying overhead, their wings flapping gracefully. She turned her head to find Sombra, looking at her with tenderness and love. Her heart skipped a beat as she smiled at him, her eyes welling up with emotion. He looked at her for a moment before walking towards her and settling by her side.

"That's a beautiful memory," he said, his voice soft and soothing.

"I miss those days," she sighed, her voice tinged with longing.

"You can always relive them within you," he reassured her.

She nodded, but her heart was heavy with doubt. "True, but..." Her voice trailed off as a tear rolled down her cheek. "I don't know if I can live without them."

His gaze softened, and he replied, "Life presents you with choices, and if you focus on what you missed out on, you'll never find joy in what you have chosen."

"But how can I forget the life I'm leaving behind? Both lives have people and places that I love, how can I possibly choose one?" she confided, her voice shaky with emotion.

He smiled, a wise and patient expression on his face. "There is no right or wrong choice. Both have sacrifices and rewards. What matters is what you think is necessary to lead a life that is right for you."

Curious, she asked, "What would you do in my position?"

His eyes twinkled mischievously as he said, "Come with me."

Guided by Sombra, her feet followed the winding path that led to the village. The world around her was alive with wonder, each step leading her deeper into the embrace of nature. The trees swayed in the breeze, their leaves rustling like the sound of distant applause, as if welcoming her home. Birds chirped and sang, their melodies weaving together into a symphony of sound that resonated deep within her soul. She felt as if she was a part of something greater, something infinite and timeless. But with every step, she couldn't help but wonder if she was ready to embrace this life forever, or if she should leave it all behind. The more she pondered over it, the more entangled her thoughts became, like a spiderweb of doubts and uncertainties.

As they walked on, the vibrant colours and scents of the

village slowly came into view, beckoning her like a distant dream. Her steps slowed to a measured pace, as she struggled to come to terms with the conflicting emotions inside her. Would she find her true purpose here, or would she forever be a wanderer, lost in the winds of fate?

Her gaze swept over the walls of their humble abode as they stepped into the berry bush, drawn to the intricate paintings adorning them. The vibrant colours seemed to pulsate with renewed energy as if each brushstroke was breathing new life into the images depicted. She marvelled at the stunning detail that had previously gone unnoticed, realizing that every stroke had been carefully crafted to convey a tale she had yet to uncover.

"My life was similar to yours," he said, gesturing towards a hidden section of the painting of a tall man who had lost his way in the jungle. He had been rescued by a creature like himself and brought to the village to heal. He found a close companion in his saviour and learned about himself while living in the jungle. "On the night of my initiation, I too was offered a choice but I chose to stay back. I left behind a successful life in the city, my loving family, and friends to become a protector of this land."

She listened intently, her eyes tracing the lines of the painting. As she gazed at it, she realised that sometimes the right choice isn't always the easiest. The man in the painting had chosen to leave behind everything he knew and loved to embrace a new life, one that was full of challenges and uncertainties. She turned towards him, her heart filled with a mix of emotions.

She knew that a difficult choice lay ahead of her.

"Did you ever regret leaving that life behind?" she asked him, her eyes searching his face for any hint of doubt.

"Never," he responded without hesitation. "But don't let my decision guide yours. Your journey is your own. I'm only sharing my experience so that you know that both paths have rewards and sacrifices. And if you embrace the choice you make without regretting the life you leave behind, that's when you'll find joy and fulfilment."

While listening to his words, she couldn't help but wonder what he looked like as a human. She was fascinated that he had gone through a similar journey to hers. As she stared at him blankly, memories of their first encounter flooded her mind. She had thought of him as a monster, someone who was out to kill her. But now, he was her closest companion and instrumental in helping her find herself.

"When did you turn into this form?" she inquired, her curiosity getting the best of her.

"Over 300 years ago," he replied calmly, unfazed by her curiosity.

Her eyes widened in amazement. "How long can you live?" she asked.

"It depends on my purpose. When I've fulfilled my purpose in this forest, my body will naturally begin to wear out, and I'll begin to age faster and eventually perish."

"If I decide to stay back, would you be with me forever?" she asked hesitantly, her heart aching at the thought of losing him.

"No one can guarantee the amount of time they are destined to give to another," he replied in a sombre tone. "Your one and only companion that will stay with you forever is yourself. But I wish to have a full life with you for as long as it is fated," he added, his eyes filled with love and tenderness.

Her heart skipped a beat as the words left her. "How would it make you feel if I decided to leave this place?" The thought of her leaving filled her with a sense of longing and dread.

"I will cherish every moment we have together and hold onto the memories of our time together once you're gone," he replied, his eyes glistening with emotion.

Her eyes welled up with tears as he spoke about their connection. "I have never felt as close to anyone else, as I have with you," she said in a soft voice. "I doubt I'll ever find that kind of connection with someone else," she added

"You possess the capacity to form an even more profound bond," he reassured her.

"With whom?" she inquired, puzzled.

"With yourself," he replied, his words soothing her. "Once you find that inner closeness, you won't feel the need to seek it outside of yourself."

He beckoned her to follow him, and she eagerly complied. Walking ahead, the landscape transformed from a lush, verdant forest to a barren wasteland, devoid of life. A sense of emptiness filled her, but she found comfort in the presence of her companion. Finally, they arrived at a tree unlike any she had ever seen before. Its branches were adorned with an unusual fruit, coloured in shades of blue and purple, that glimmered in the sunlight. The tree was the only sign of life in this desolate land, but it was enough to fill her with a sense of wonder and hope.

"Decades ago, a massive fire ravaged this section of the forest. The once-thriving ecosystem had been reduced to a smouldering wasteland, devoid of any life or vitality. However, hope sprouted from the ashes in the form of a small, delicate plant. The villagers, eager to help the forest recover, wished to nurture the plant into a mighty tree that could breathe life back into the desolate land. But Guaia forbade them from intervening, she believed that if the plant was meant to thrive, it would do so on its own, without any external help. And so the villagers, reluctantly but obediently, heeded her words and left the plant to its own devices. Years passed, and the once-tiny plant had grown into a towering, magnificent tree, its branches stretching out towards the sky, the only beacon of life in the barren land. The tree stood proud and resilient, unfazed by the emptiness around it, for it knew that it had accomplished the impossible, all on its own."

As she listened to the tale of the bountiful tree, she couldn't help but marvel at its strength and determination. She thought about the times in her life when she had felt lost and alone, searching for a sense of belonging outside of herself.

"Often we are faced with such situations in our own lives when we are left in a place where there is nothing around us, no family, no friends, no support," he continued to ease Aaliyah's dilemma. "We lose our sense of belonging because there is nothing that resonates with our principles. In those moments, we can either choose to give up, blame our destiny for being unfair, and resort to attaching ourselves to people and situations that may be harmful to us, or we can choose to go inward and find a sense of belonging inside. Trying to find a sense of belonging outside will always lead to disappointment because, unless you have embraced your own being completely, you will never know who you truly are. When you go inward and find a sense of belonging within, you will stop seeking it outside."

"I know that feeling of disappointment too well," she said while trailing off into another thought. "This is the first time in my life when I feel content with my life, it feels like I've lived a full life here even though I've only been here for a few weeks. But my life back in the city feels incomplete. I feel it would be unfair to my family if I leave them now when they are getting older and may need my support. I need to be with them and mend my relationships."

"Whatever choice you make, remember to let go of the attachment you have to the life you're leaving behind because those attachments will never allow you to be fully content with what you have," Sombra advised

She took a deep breath, knowing that she would find her way, just like the resilient tree that had grown against all odds. Neither of the two choices was easy, but she had the clarity to know what she needed to choose.

Reunion

Approaching the source tree, Sombra's voice carried a hint of admiration as he remarked, "You've chosen well."

Aaliyah walked with a determined stride towards Guaia, who was seated in solitary meditation. She nestled herself at the wise woman's feet, seeking her guidance. Together they sat in a comfortable silence, watching the sun slowly dip behind the trees, casting magnificent shadows that filled the clearing with a surreal beauty.

As the evening set in, the clearing slowly filled up with residents. The hum of the village, with residents exchanging goods and laughter, was like a lullaby to Aaliyah's ears. Looking around, she couldn't help but marvel at the ethereal charm of the place. She felt a tug in her heart, knowing that she would miss it dearly. "Are you certain about your decision?" Guaia asked, sensing her restlessness.

"I'm certain," she responded, slightly hesitant but firm, assuring the wise woman that she had made up her mind.

"Then you have my blessings," said Guaia, placing her hand on Aaliyah and Sombra's faces.

While embarking on their journey to the holy lake, she felt reassured by her choice and comforted by Sombra's company. However, the crowd at the marketplace soon swallowed them up, and she found herself searching for him amidst the sea of faces.

While crawling through the crowd, she looked up and saw a tall, chiselled man in front of her, presenting her with traditional white drapes. His amber-gold eyes sparkled in the light, and she couldn't help but notice how perfect he looked. In return for the drapes, she embraced the stranger, feeling grateful for his unexpected kindness. After they parted ways, she continued her journey towards the holy lake, feeling a renewed sense of calm.

"Where is he?" she wondered, her eyes longing to see that dark figure one last time before he would turn into a human.

When she finally arrived, the holy lake was just as beautiful as she remembered it to be. The soft, azure glow of the water calmed her nerves, but she was still unsure of why Sombra had left her alone. Hoping he would return soon, she decided to settle by the shore, her eyes fixed on the brilliant stars twinkling in the night sky. She took in every moment, revelling in the quietude of the moment. Looking up at the arm of the Milky Way stretching across the sky, her eyes grew heavy with sleep. She lay down on the ground, feeling the soft earth beneath her body. The sky was a painting, and she couldn't resist the urge to capture every detail before she had to leave this magical place. Slowly, she drifted into slumber, cradled by the calm and serene atmosphere of the holy lake.

A gentle, soothing touch awakened her. Gradually opening her eyes, she beheld a radiant face staring back at her. As her eyes adjusted to the dim light, she found herself locked in a captivating gaze with an ethereal being seated in front of her. The emerald eyes that stared at her were like a portal to another world, brimming with raw emotion and depth. Her heart fluttered as she continued to gaze into those eyes, feeling like she could get lost in them forever.

Finally, breaking the spell, she pulled herself out of the trance and noticed the striking features of the face in front of her. She had never seen a face so perfect. The nose was sharp and straight, while the lips were narrow yet full, with a hint of depression on the cheek. The smile that appeared on his face was so perfect that it almost seemed unreal. It revealed perfectly aligned, pearly white teeth that added to the already dazzling smile. As he leaned in to place a gentle kiss on her forehead, she was overcome with a flood of emotions. She felt that warm, comforting presence that was her strength in this forest.

The touch of his lips on her forehead felt like a blessing, and she found herself wishing that this moment could last forever. She savoured the moment, taking in every detail of this vision in front of her because now their time together was limited. She held him close in a tight embrace, feeling the warmth of his body and a surge of love that made her insides melt with desire. Enveloped in Sombra's broad, muscular arms, she surrendered to the moment, allowing herself to be lost in a reverie where they could be together forever. She felt safe and secure in his embrace as if nothing else in the world mattered except for the two of them.

Slowly opening her eyes, she found herself sleeping alone beside the tranquil lake with the morning sun filtering through the towering trees. Confused and disoriented, she looked around, wondering if her encounter with Sombra had been nothing more than a vivid dream. Suddenly, she heard the sound of footsteps approaching from behind. Turning around, she found herself face-to-face with the stunning man she had dreamed of. He looked even more radiant in the golden glow of the sun, with his chiselled features, intense gaze, and long, sculpted fingers holding a bunch of ripe passion fruits. She smiled at him, her heart beating wildly with excitement and joy. "You're so beautiful," she said softly, taking a bite of the juicy passion fruit from his hand. He returned her smile with a look of love and tenderness, making her feel like she was the only person in the world that mattered to him. With a smile on her face, she looked into his eyes, feeling a sense of awe and wonder at the mysterious, alluring man who had captured her heart. At that moment, she knew that she had found her soulmate and that nothing would ever be the same again.

As she gently tugged his luscious brown hair behind his ears, she looked at him with a warm smile and asked, "How do you feel?"

"Taller," he responded with a gentle chuckle.

"I'm sorry, I can't stop staring at your face. I don't think I've ever seen anyone so beautiful," she said, with a smile on her face. He gently rested his hand on her cheek, warming her insides.

"Come, let's go to the village," he urged, taking her hand and leading her towards the village.

"Did you look like this when you were human?" she asked.

"I don't remember what I looked like in that life, and I don't know what I look like now," he replied, his eyes focused on the path ahead of them.

"Didn't you look at yourself in the lake?" she inquired.

"It didn't matter. What mattered was how you perceived me, and that was enough," he explained, his eyes briefly meeting hers.

"But aren't you even slightly curious about your appearance?" She prodded, her curiosity getting the better of her.

"Not at all. If I am meant to see my reflection, I will come across it in one way or another," he answered, his gaze focused on the path once again.

"Does it feel weird to be in this form after so many years?" she asked, trying to imagine what it would feel like to not know what you looked like.

"Not really. Guaia and my life in this village have helped me detach from the exterior. As long as I am able to preserve my inner peace and nurture the world within, my external form doesn't matter," he replied, his voice calm and serene. She looked at him in awe, marvelling at his wisdom.

"Do you remember any part of your life as a human?" she asked, her curiosity still not satiated.

"Faintly," he replied, "it seems like a very distant dream."

"Do you remember anything about your family or where you lived?" she asked, hoping to gain some insight into his past.

"I have a hazy memory of a woman and maybe a young child. I don't recall anything beyond that,"

"Did you ever miss them or think about them after you decided to stay back here?" she asked, wondering how he coped with leaving everything behind.

"I don't remember, but I learned an important lesson about relationships during my early days here. Every relationship we build in our lives has a purpose and a timeline. If we try to hang on to those relationships beyond the time they are meant to be with us, it brings us nothing but grief and disappointment. If we embrace that relationship for the time it is meant to be with us and then let go of it when it's meant to leave us, we will be at peace," his voice filled with wisdom.

She pondered his words, reflecting on her own experiences with holding on to relationships past their expiration date, which only left her with emotional scars.

Walking towards the village, she felt gratitude for the wisdom he shared with her. Maybe she was meant to leave her city life behind, which is why she experienced all that she did in this forest.

Had she chosen wrong?

The doubts crept slowly into her conscience, and she began to question her choices. She had a tendency to hold onto things that no longer served her, whether in memories or in the physical, and she wondered if she was doing the same thing again.

The colourful and vibrant bazaar slowly came into view as they walked in silence. The bustling marketplace was filled with a medley of aromas that wafted through the air, causing the senses to come alive. The earthy scent of cumin, mixed with the fiery aroma of chilli peppers, was making her sweat, while the sweet floral notes of vanilla, combined with the refreshing hints of peppermint, were calming her soul. The market was truly a feast for the senses. The sound of drums and laughter echoed through the market, adding to the festive ambience.

"Is there something special today?" Aaliyah enquired

"This is how the residents celebrate transitional phases." He told her, "This is organised for our last day together." Those last three words were like a red-hot branding iron to her heart. Why was this regret creeping in? she wondered. Was she done with her life back in the city? Was this the life she was meant to choose?

Sombra pulled her into the crowd of merrymakers and swayed her to the beat of the drum. His firm yet gentle grip on her, his woody fragrance, and his broad, protective chest made her forget all her worries, and she gave in to the celebrations. She closed her eyes, gave into his grip, and moved to the music vibrating through the forest floor.

"I want to sit for some time," said Aaliyah, walking away from the party. He promptly followed her, and they settled next to a passion fruit tree. She leaned on his shoulder.

"I don't know if I made the right decision," she confessed, her voice laced with uncertainty.

"Maybe I was meant to leave my city life behind, which is why I experienced all that I did in this forest."

He placed a reassuring hand on her shoulder. "There is always a reason why we choose what we do. If you don't lose sight of why you made the choice, your journey will be meaningful."

Looking into his emerald eyes, she asked, "But what if I was wrong?"

"Every path, every choice, can help your growth. Now that you have made this decision, you need to focus on what you can learn from it instead of regretting what you'll miss out on if you had made another choice," he advised kindly.

She sighed and sank into his shoulder while staring blankly at the crowd, getting lost in their merriment.

"How do you stay connected to your purpose when there is so much happening around?" she asked, her eyes never leaving the crowd.

"You can learn to let it float away, just like a feather in the wind. What do you think will happen if you were to attach yourself to everything you see around you?" he asked.

"I will lose my own way," she replied.

"Correct! But if you just focus on what you have and the next step, not only will you enjoy your journey, but you will also learn from every step," he said with a smile.

She looked up at him with tears in her eyes.

"I kept thinking about leaving behind my home and my life back in the city, but I never realised that this place has been more of a home for me than any other place. I have never felt more at one with myself before this. I had been chasing a sense of home my entire life, and I didn't recognize it when I found it."

"I'll tell you a secret," he said with a mischievous grin.

"Your home is inside you. If you find your sense of belonging within, then any place can become home."

"I wish you had told me this secret before I made my decision," she said with a small smile.

"Everything happens for a reason, dear Lali," he said, using the childhood nickname Aaliyah's mother used to call her. Hearing him call her Lali was like a journey back to her childhood, and she was amazed at how much he knew about her. "Everything you ever need is right here," he said as he placed his warm hands on her heart.

"Find yourself, trust yourself, and you will always find your home."

Cycle

Transfixed with the beauty of the moment, Aaliyah looked on with her eyes fixed on the horizon as the sun slowly set, casting an orange and pink hue across the sky. He sat beside her, holding her hand and admiring the view. The dispersing crowd around them seemed to fade into the background as they watched the beautiful sunset.

Suddenly, he turned to her and whispered, "There is one thing left to do." She looked up at him, her heart pounding with anticipation.

She knew that their time together was coming to an end, and the thought of leaving this world behind filled her with sadness. "What is it?" she asked softly.

He took her hand and led her back towards the lake. She knew that at this moment, nothing else mattered except being with him. She couldn't believe how quickly the day ended, and she was nearing the end of her time with him. Tears streamed down her face as she thought about leaving this world behind. His presence was all she cared for, no matter what form he was in. It was the warmth she needed—nothing else.

Lifting her up, he ran through the forest, trying to distract her from her thoughts. She laughed and released herself from his grip and ran around the trees, trying to dodge him, while he tried to chase her. Their innocent laughter filled the forest as they approached the lake. Finally, as they arrived at the lake, Sombra removed his drapes, motioning Aaliyah to join him in the water. She hesitated for a moment before disrobing herself and clasping his hand.

As they waded into the water, she felt the energy of the lake flowing through her body. It was as if every cell in her body was waking up. She closed her eyes and let the warmth of the lake envelop her. As they reached the middle of the lake, they faced each other, the stars above glistening over the water. The silence was only interrupted by the soft sounds of the water and the gentle breeze. She inched closer to him, and he placed a gentle kiss on her lips. She felt his warmth fill her insides, while the warmth of the lake climbed up to her temple. They lost themselves in each other's embrace, slowly sinking into the pull of the lake.

Descending deeper into the water, she felt herself becoming one with him and the energy web surrounding them. She couldn't see him as a separate entity but as a part of her being. They floated together in the bright green lattice exploring themselves in each other. Finally, as they emerged from the water, the entire forest glowed bright green with their love. They shared a passionate kiss, and for a moment, everything else seemed to disappear. Time felt like it had slowed down as they inched towards the edge of the lake. All the doubts and worries that were nagging Aaliyah had disappeared for those moments they were in the lake.

They wore their garments and decided to lie down by the lake to spend whatever little time they had left together. She felt full of emotions and love for herself, Sombra, and the forest and wanted to focus on relishing this magical moment.

She put her head on Sombra's muscular arms and looked into his deep emerald eyes, "I love you," she whispered. His earthy fragrance and warm embrace comforted her, and she felt blessed to have experienced this life."I wish I had chosen differently," a thought lingered at a far distance, and a slight lump began to build up in her throat. She allowed the thought to float away and focused on being in the moment. She closed her eyes and buried herself in his broad, protective chest.

She focused on the soft, grassy bed beneath her and the warm embrace, wishing that the moment would last forever. The beautiful bird song in the distance and the sound of the soft breeze blowing through the trees were slowly fading into the gentle, rhythmic ring that rose from her side. As the ring grew louder, her arm stretched out in response to grab the source. With closed eyes, she fiddled with it, and a familiar voice screamed from the other end.

"Pack your bags, we're going to the Amazon!"

9 789359 168708